CAPTOR
CAPTIVE

The Intense, Psychological Suspense Thriller

L.J. Kane

Bentley Hereford Publishing

UNITED KINGDOM

Published by: Bentley Hereford Publishing
United Kingdom

Publisher's Note: This is a work of fiction. Names, characters, places, and incidents are a product of the author's imagination. Locales and public names are sometimes used for atmospheric purposes. Any resemblance to actual people, living or dead, or to businesses, companies, events, institutions, or locales is completely coincidental.

Book Layout © 2014 BookDesignTemplates.com

Book Cover Artist: SelfPubBookCovers.com/INeedABookCover

Publishing Company Logo Design: logaster.com

Author Website: http://ljkaneauthor.wordpress.com

Captor Captive/L.J. Kane – Second edition. Originally published as Snatch Girl by L.J. Kane.

ISBN: 978-0-9956273-6-9

CONTENTS

CHAPTER ONE

BREATHE

A shapeless shadow lunged from the semi-darkness, pitching her to the floor, with its solid weight on top of her, as Ellie pushed open her front door. She squealed as her head smacked against the hall table, with the blood from her split brow spattering across her forehead, her body overpowered by his strength, and her senses overpowered by his vile stench of sweat.

Ellie screamed and writhed, face down beneath him, as he slammed the door, and forced her face against the cold, hard tiles, tearing her college bag from her shoulder, and snatching her phone from her hand, hurling them across the floor.

He pinned her arms behind her back, with her shoulder blades burning, and the ice-cold metal biting into her flesh as the handcuffs snapped shut around her wrists, trapping her stinging, bleeding skin, Ellie kicking and thrashing, her body shaking beneath his weight as he held her down.

"Let me go. For Christ's sake, let me go, you bastard. What are you doing to me?" She curled her hands into fists, yanking her wrists apart, but the handcuffs held firm, with the rough, metal edges cutting into her skin. "Help me, somebody, help me." The pitch in her voice rose to a scream as fear tightened her throat.

He wrenched her onto her back and straddled her, smothering her, with his thumb and finger sealing her nose, and his calloused palm crushing her lips, stifling her harrowing screams. The claustrophobic vacuum constricted her throat as she gasped in vain for air, her back arching, her heels drumming against the floor, and her lungs burning. *Somebody help me. Please help me. Oh, God. What's happening? What's going on?*

He tugged a damp, sweet-smelling cloth from his pocket, bunching it in his hand. He let go of her for a second, and in that moment of freedom, Ellie took a deep breath and held it. The cloth came over her face like a crushing mask, Ellie clawing at the shackles beneath her trembling body, with her eyes wide, and her heart palpitating. *Oh God, no. No.*

The sweet smell of chloroform fought for supremacy over his body odour, her stomach jolting with every dry retch, and her eyes streaming, Ellie nauseated by the spinning sensation inside her head. *Don't breathe, Ellie, don't breathe.*

He pulled her up from the floor, and dragged her backwards through the hallway, with the heels of her boots scuffing the tiles as Ellie squirmed in his vice-like grip, wrenching the handcuffs clamped between her wrists. *Come home, Doug, please. I need you. What's happening to me?*

Their reflections edged into the hall mirror, Ellie lurching at the sight of her blue eyes wide open in terror, her pale blonde hair streaked with blood, with her tanned complexion, ghost-like. The bloodstained cloth obscured her face, with her cheeks pushed in by the pressure of his hand as the blood from her split brow trickled over his fingers. Gone – the flirtatious glint in her eye. Missing, the teasing grin she kept for the boys. Her captor's dark, soulless eyes stared back at her through the mirror, and Ellie's veins iced up as his lip curled into a snarl.

"Breathe in, you bitch."

He shouldered the door open with a thud, the door swinging wide, and then swinging back, hitting her leg before slamming shut, cutting off the haunting image as he dragged her into the kitchen. She felt the cold rush of air from an open door, and her heart jolted at the sound of a car starting up outside, its engine revving, impatient and loud. Her stomach tightened, pulling inwards, and her lungs ached as she choked beneath his hand.

"Breathe, you dumb bitch." He drove his fist into her stomach, Ellie expelling the air with a rush, with an unbelievable hollow pain spearing her gut, her body folding, crumpling, and her head falling forward, inhalation imminent, and inevitable. *Oh, God.*

He dragged her outside, the revving louder now, with the icy wind curling around her, piercing every inch of her wilting body. He tried to lift her as the car door clicked open, and Ellie lifted her head, mustering the last of her strength, with her jaw tight, and her skin clammy.

She raised her knee to her chest, then rammed the heel of her boot into his groin, crushing, digging in, with his testicles banging together beneath her foot. He gave an agonised howl, and fell to his knees, his teeth clenched, and his face contorted, with the cloth falling from his grasp.

Ellie sprawled onto the frozen ground, gasping, dazed, with her body weak, and breathless. She tore at the handcuffs, clawing at the metal link between them, her nails breaking and bleeding. She had to run, had to escape, but with her hands behind her, and no strength in her legs, she couldn't even push herself up from the ground. Even as she cried for help, the tightness in her chest strangled her voice, and her words carried no more than a few feet. *Oh shit.*

Ellie raised her head in hope at the sound of running footsteps, and as the man reached her, he slowed to a stop, car keys in hand. He glanced down at her captor kneeling with his forehead against the earth, gripping his crotch, and then he switched his gaze to Ellie, his windswept brown hair falling across his brow, his face familiar, attractive, with the most hypnotic brown eyes.

His fingers curled around her shoulder, gripping, tightening, and then he hauled her to her knees, with his fist raised. Ellie gasped, her heart shrinking within her chest as she realised then that he was party to her kidnap. *Oh no, please, no.*

He watched as the tears trickled down Ellie's bloodied cheeks, and as she begged him to free her, he closed his eyes and hit her. The murderous ache swelled inside her head, the rapid darkening of her vision reducing the man to a silhouette, pitched against the blue-black winter sky, and as the scene faded to black, her heavy eyelids closed, and Ellie slumped against his legs, lying crumpled and vulnerable at his feet.

She didn't feel him lift her, she didn't feel the cold leather of the rear seat on which he lay her down, nor did she feel the car shake a little as he sat in the driver's seat, next to her injured captor whose vile threats towards her disappeared into the void. If she'd heard his threats, she would have thrown herself from the car into the path of another.

CHAPTER TWO

AMBIVALENCE

The hard stone floor stirred her, Ellie trembling in the darkness, woozy, dazed, as she drifted in and out of a dreamlike state, her naked body wet from the dank cellar floor, her eyes open but unseeing, her limbs heavy, and her fingers crippled with cold.

The putrid smell of rat urine and stale beer seeped into her nose and down her throat, Ellie drooling and retching as her awareness returned. The effects of the anaesthetic, her only saviour from Jon Braddon's twisted mind, faded into the darkness as she curled her shivering body into a tight ball, clenching her stomach, with her heart thudding. *Oh God, I'm still here.*

A dull ache sat low within her abdomen, with her inner thighs bruised, and her breasts tender. She knew that Braddon's perverse, sexual needs were intensifying with Ellie powerless to resist his abuse, while she lay drugged with anaesthetics as he emulated her death, building towards his ultimate goal.

Then the cycle would begin again – Braddon waking her, his phone in his hand, playing videos of naked women writhing in agony beneath their abusers, the women begging, pleading, as they bled to death from deep wounds cut into their wrists. Their fading screams wrenched Ellie's guts, chilling her soul as Braddon paused and replayed, over and over, his smile widening and his body odour strengthening with his arousal, as Ellie's uncontrollable tears ran down her cheeks. Then he'd drug her to abuse her, and then she'd awaken, a while later, wretched and dirty, like now.

Ellie sobbed in the darkness, awaiting Braddon's final descent into the cellar with a knife. Her stomach twisted, knotting tight, with her breath lodging in her tightening throat as she imagined the excruciating pain of her skin splitting open, the blade digging around in her wrist before slitting her veins, her blood draining and pooling around her, Braddon thrusting, with Ellie dying beneath him. *Oh God. Why me? What did I do?*

A sudden cough came from deep within the shadows, and Ellie froze, chills spreading through her veins like crystallized ice. The tip of an unseen cigarette burned red in the darkness, and then it brightened as its owner took a long drag.

Ellie heard movement in the cellar, footsteps striding over to the right, and then glass clinking against metal. Ellie squeezed her eyes closed as the light flickered on, blinding bright white against the dark shadow of her closed eyelids.

The man drew breath, and as Ellie opened her eyes, she saw him in silhouette, standing a few feet away, and then he stepped back, looking down at her as he steadied the swinging light-shade. She saw him beneath the light, with his black studded boots and blue jeans speckled with fresh mud, a silver biker's buckle on his leather belt, and the sleeves of his casual shirt rolled up to the elbow, a mobile phone crammed into his left breast pocket, and a packet of cigarettes in the other. He took a drag, and then dropped the cigarette, squashing it to a pulp with his foot.

He came forward, his hand cold against her wet skin as he reached down for her arm, and she cowered from him, remembering his fist driving down on her, to aid Braddon's kidnap attempt, two or three days ago. Ellie dared to look up into his keen brown eyes as he tugged her to her feet, his voice shattering the silence, his Australian accent distinct yet familiar.

"What did Braddon drug you with?" He gripped her as she wavered and he shook her. "Answer me."

"I don't know. Don't shake me like that." Ellie's slurred speech startled her. She swiped at his arm. "Let go of me, you bastard."

She wrenched herself from his hold, falling to the floor, crying out as her hip struck the corner of the raised flagstone beneath her. She rolled onto her back, cradling her hip, sucking air through her clenched teeth as the pains radiated through her bones like shock-waves from a hammer blow.

He fended off her weak punches as he came for-ward, his weight bearing down on her bruised legs as he knelt on her thighs, Ellie's feeble pushes too weak to move him. He gripped her wrists, and then yanked her towards him, his face close to hers, his eyes pierc-ing.

"Braddon's upstairs, trippin', took crack or some-thin'," he said. "If you hit me again, I'll fetch him. D'you want that?"

Ellie gasped, shaking her head, the heavy weight of anxiety crushing her chest as he slid off her, and then he pushed his arm around her waist and hooked his other arm behind her knees. He lifted her with ease and carried her to the cellar steps, setting her down on the third step from the bottom, Ellie gasping, the cold stone sharp to her naked buttocks.

Her knee trembled against his leg as he placed his hand on her thigh, and as he ran his hand down to her knee and added pressure, the shaking stopped, but El-lie's stomach turned over. She looked up into his eyes, and then shrank back as the flicker of a leer passed over his face.

"Don't you dare touch me." She closed her fingers around his wrist and tugged hard, but she couldn't move it, with her loose grip, and her fingers tingling. He plucked her fingers from his wrist, crushing her other hand as she threw him a feeble punch, Ellie's face creasing as pains shot through her fingers.

"I warned you, Ellie," he said. "I'll fetch him if you fight me."

Ellie snatched her hands from his hold, her tears welling up again, with her fingers throbbing. She rubbed her wrist, a red mark appearing where he'd held it, and she kicked out at his legs as he reached for her shoulder.

Her skin tingled all over, and she retched, Ellie gasping and swallowing, taking deep breaths, and then she retched again with her hand to her mouth. *Oh shit. Don't let me be sick again.* Acid burned like a shot of whiskey at the back of her throat, and then it sank back down when she gulped, leaving her throat feeling raw.

The man took a quick step back, with his jaw set. "How long ago did you come to?" he said. "Did he reverse the drug, or did you just wake up? Did you throw up?"

"Why should you care?" Tears threatened to burst out, and she turned her head away, swallowing hard, wiping the tears from her eyes with the back of her hand. "You left me here with him. You just drove off, and you didn't come back."

"No. I was just the getaway driver. Job done. That dickhead screwed up the snatch, and I had to smack your head. You shouldn't have seen me," he said. "I'm here now. Get used to it."

Ellie eyed him, biting the inside of her lip, shrinking back as he came forward. "Please don't touch me," she said.

He gave her a withering stare, Ellie flinching as he placed his hand beneath her chin, peering into each of her eyes, and then felt the pulse in her neck, glancing over her bruised hip. Ellie covered her crotch with her hands as he glanced down, and then he lifted his gaze to her face, pausing at her breasts, Ellie searching his expression for a sign of compassion, but found him difficult to read. Gaps still littered her thinking and her memories. His accent and undoubtable attractiveness had no place right now within her disconnected memories, but she knew that they should. *I should know this bloody man.*

Ellie jerked her head away as he pushed her hair off her face and examined the dried cut to her forehead. Her heart raced and her tears brimmed.

"For God's sake, stop touching me," she said. "Just go. Leave me alone. I . . . I can't cope with this."

He slipped his hands into the pockets of his jeans, and then leaned back against the wall. "Beaut, I'm not gonna hurt you. I know what he's done to you, and I know what he's plannin'—"

"He told you?"

He shook his head. "No. He's filmed it, all of it. I saw it, pictures, sound, everythin'." He looked away. "It's on the internet. He sent the link to your stepfather, about an hour ago."

"Oh God, no, not to Doug." The bile rose from the depths of her stomach and burned her chest inside. She choked as the acid entered her throat and she forced it back down, with her hands clenched in her lap. "Please tell me you're lying, please say it's all lies."

"D'you see the camera?" He turned, pointing towards the far corner of the ceiling. "It's OK." He turned back to face her. "It can't film you now."

Ellie peered around him at the tiny camera hanging from the ceiling joist, her eyes widening, and her lower lip trembling. She guessed, from its angle, that every part of the room was visible, with every action recorded in its entirety for the world to see and hear – Braddon's rages, the drugging, the degrading abuse, Ellie squatting for a pee. Ellie's mind reeled, and she retched again. *This isn't happening.*

She tried to stand, but toppled forwards, crying out as she fell, scraping the skin from her shins on the edge of the steps. He caught her before she could hit the floor, and then he guided her back onto the step, peering at her grazed legs as he crouched in front of her. Ellie sobbed, holding her shins, with the burning sensation too much to bear.

A sudden noise from the floor above stole his attention from her, and he put her aside, with his expression grim, and his fist clenched. He ascended the steps with Ellie staggering after him, and then he shut the door in her face, locking the cellar door behind him.

"Damn you," Ellie yelled. She thumped the door with her fists, but his footsteps faded fast, and she slumped against the wall, her body crumpling, with her limbs shaking. "Damn you," she said, half to herself.

She slid down the wall, her shoulder blades scraping against the abrasive brickwork, and she landed with a thud on the top step. Her smarting shins surpassed the pain in her hip, and Ellie burst into tears. She kept her face turned away from the camera, and let the unchecked tears flow.

Muffled sounds came from above for a while, then a door slammed and then silence. Ellie listened to the continuous dripping, which accompanied every living moment in the cellar, and the rats, scurrying between the beer barrels in search of scraps. The sharp crack of Braddon's inhumane animal trap sent a spear of anguish through her heart as another defenceless creature succumbed to Braddon's brutal reign. She wiped away her tears with the heels of her hands, and then closed her eyes, with her arms folded around her knees, hugging them close. *Why me? What have I done wrong? What did I do?*

She must have slept, for when she raised her head the wooziness had cleared, and her buttocks were numb. Ellie gasped, with her heart in her mouth, as the door swung open, and she scrambled to her feet, scraping her elbow on the wall beside her. The man reappeared in the doorway, Ellie crouching in the corner, praying that Braddon wouldn't walk in behind him.

She nursed her elbow, covering her crotch with her hand as the man looked down at her. He walked in and closed the door, signalling to her to move down the steps, and as Ellie reached the bottom, he threw down a bag of clothes, and then tossed her a hot, wet sponge wrapped in a small towel.

"We're leavin'," he said. "Just me and you. Sponge yourself down, then get dressed, and keep quiet."

Ellie held back the tears as the man watched her, Ellie eyeing him, with her hands trembling. *I'll be OK. He's letting me dress, and he's taking me home.*

She turned her back on him to sponge away the stale beer, water, and traces of blood, washing away the stench of Braddon's sweat from her skin. She sensed the man's gaze on her as she dried her damp, shivering body on the tiny towel, the rough fabric scratching her tender skin.

To her relief, the clothes in the bag were her own, and she pulled out her underwear, slipping the pretty little knickers on first, shutting out his roving eye. Her jeans followed, but her bra was missing.

She turned to face him, zipping up her jeans, then fastening the button. "Where's my bra?"

"Dunno." His gaze didn't stray from her bare breasts, and she guessed that the thought of finding her bra was the furthest from his mind.

Ellie jerked, with her heart thudding, as a flashback played out in front of her eyes, of Braddon's dirty, nicotine-stained fingers tearing open her bra, then dragging her knickers down her bare legs as she begged him to stop. Memories of Braddon drooling at the sight of her lips, with his hot breath on her crotch as he molested her with his tongue, her thighs trembling as Braddon held open her legs, with her arms shackled behind her. She heaved as she forced the vile memory into the deepest pocket of her mind, forever grateful for the anaesthetics that blanked out the rest of the abuse.

She looked up at his getaway driver, standing at the top of the steps, the shiver creeping over her shoulders as he withdrew his hands from his pockets and folded his arms, staring down at her with a glint in his eye.

"Please find my bra," Ellie said.

"Forget your bra. I'm not headin' back for it. Put your sweater on."

He stooped, picked up her boots from the floor beside him, and threw them down to her, Ellie dodging them with a squeal as they fell around her, splashing into the puddles of stale beer, with tiny speckles appearing on the legs of her favourite jeans.

She sat on the step with her back to him, the soft, cashmere sweater clinging to her figure as she slipped it on, then freed her long hair from the neck. She sponged the beer from the soles of her feet, wiping them dry with the towel, before she pulled on her woollen socks, and then her boots, with the faux fur lining warming her freezing feet. She spread her toes out, enveloped in warmth and softness.

"Come here," he said. "Braddon's upstairs and I don't wanna leave without you."

Ellie looked up, holding onto the handrail to steady herself. "I'm going home?"

He straightened. "No."

"You're not taking me home?" The back of her neck tingled, and she heaved herself to her feet, backing off as he started down the stairs after her. "Where are you taking me?" she said. "I'm not going with you if you won't take me home."

He reached her, then seized her shoulder, leaning in close, his voice low. "He'll kill you, Ellie."

Ellie clutched at the handrail, lightheaded and nauseous. He prized her hand from the rail, and she backed away, banging into the wall, with her chest tight and her breathing fast.

"Where are you taking me?" she said. "Why have you come back? What's happening?"

"Are you comin' with me or have I got to knock you out?" He advanced, and she put out her hand to stop him, but he walked right into her, and crushed her against the wall, trapping her other arm behind her back. Ellie held her breath, then cringed as his lips brushed her ear. "You play me up," he whispered, "and I'll hurt you. You don't wanna stay here alone with him, do you?"

Ellie gaped. "No. Don't leave me with him, please. I'll . . . I'll come with you."

He yanked her away from the wall, with a firm grip on her arm as he propelled her up the steps, with her knees stiff, and her legs aching as he marched her through the door, and into the sparse kitchen above. His fingers tightened as she recoiled at the sight of the hunting knives, fanned out on the table, with snares and animal traps piled around them, next to a soldering iron, with an unwound extension lead, long enough to reach into the cellar. *Oh shit, oh my God.* Her stomach lurched, and she froze, with a cry fleeing her lips.

He clamped his hand over her mouth, with his urgent whisper finding her ear. "He doesn't know I'm takin' you out of here. I wanna keep it that way."

Ellie nodded, her chin trembling as he led her through room after empty room of the disused inn, his eyes alert, and his jaw clenched, with the dust flying as he banged open the doors, the floor sticky underfoot as Ellie limped beside him, trying to match his fast-paced stride. He pushed her onwards, holding her around her waist, with the fingers of his other hand squeezing her arm, pushing against her contraceptive implant, Ellie feeling queasy, her lips pressed together as she fought the urge to vomit.

He smacked open a door with his palm, hauling her into a corridor with the exit door ajar at the end, blowing in the wind. Ellie gave a sudden cry as she stumbled to her knees, and as he tried to lift her, his cold hand slid under her sweater, enclosing her breast with her nipple pressing against his palm. Ellie screamed and tore from his hold, swinging her clenched fist into his stomach, and he staggered back with a yell, stalling for a second. He stared her down as he started forward, with his eyes hard, and his fist raised. Ellie backed into an alcove, banging into the locked door behind her as she cowered in the corner, shielding her head with her arms as she sank to her knees.

"Don't hurt me. Don't hurt me."

"Come here, you little shit."

He yanked her out of the recess, grappling with her, and as Ellie punched him in the chest, and broke free, he hooked his foot around her ankle and tripped her. Ellie fell full length, biting the inside of her cheek as her chin met the floor, her body jarred, and her teeth crashing together.

He hauled her up, Ellie screaming as he heaved her through the doorway into the bitter November wind that raged, unseen, around them in the night. He slapped her face. Jarring, cruel, needless, and it hurt. He slapped her again, Ellie's screams drowning out the wind as he dragged her to the car. The ice-cold metal chilled her back through her clothes as he crowded her against the side of the car, and opened the front passenger door. Just a look from him silenced her.

A movement caught her eye, and Ellie's hand raced to her mouth as Jon Braddon watched, hunched over, from an upstairs window, Ellie's gut lurching. Her new captor shot Braddon a mere glance, then forced Ellie into the passenger seat, before locking her inside the car.

Ellie shook as she searched for the door release switch on the dashboard, but he gave her no time to escape, for he was inside the car before Ellie found it. He smacked her hand away and turned the key, with the engine firing. Ellie turned her eyes away from him as he maneuvered the car through the grounds, and then he drove her away from the inn. *Where are we going? What's he going to do to me? And who the hell is he? I know him. I know I do. Oh Ellie, think.*

Dead leaves swirled passed the car, whipping into the darkness beyond, as the lane gave way to an empty main road, and then the car accelerated hard, throwing Ellie back in her seat. She saw the gear change for the tight bend, the hedges hurtling passed, and then the sudden appearance of a long, grey layby, and a mound of gravel dumped within.

The man brought the car to a shuddering stop, ripping on the handbrake, as Ellie hit the door release switch, the dashboard racing towards her as inertia threw her forwards, Ellie feeling the colour draining from her cheeks. He lunged at her, snatching her hand from the door pull, his other arm around her neck, holding her steadfast against him.

"You bloody stupid bitch."

"You're hurting me, let go of me." Ellie punched his arm, digging her nails into his shoulder, wrenching at his hand. "You're hurting me."

"I'll bloody hurt you."

He pulled the handcuffs from the door pocket, Ellie scratching, biting, and punching him as he fought for her wrists. He drew back his fist, then winded her, Ellie slumping forward with a groan, her body folding over his fist, and her guts aching. He pulled her arms in front of her, snapping on the handcuffs before he eased her back into her seat, then pulled the door shut, holding her down as he leaned over her. With a shock, she remembered where she'd met him before.

Ellie pushed him off, breathless, her words a mere whisper. "You bastard."

"Do you want me to turn the car around and take you straight back to Braddon?" He thrust the gear lever into first and spun the steering wheel, turning the car in an arc. Ellie squealed, pulling his hand from the wheel, the car jerking to a stop, and the engine stalling.

"No Darren, for God's sake."

He shot her a knowing look, then restarted the engine. "Took you long enough to remember me."

He steered into the layby, the car skidding over the rough gravelled surface before it stopped with a lurch, Ellie swiping at him as he strapped her into her seat, the pain shooting through her knuckles as they made contact with his chiseled jawbone.

He jerked his head. "For Christ's sake. You little shit."

"You bastard. Let me go." She shrank away as he glared at her, with his hand clenched, Ellie cringing, waiting for the crushing blow.

His eyes narrowed, and he lowered his fist. "You need me, Ellie. Braddon will come after you. He knows you're with me, thanks to you screamin' like a kid. You should have kept quiet."

"You groped my breast." Ellie wrenched at the handcuffs but they held fast, and he gripped the cuffs, holding her still.

"If I'd meant to grope you, I'd have felt more than your tit. Grow up, Ellie." He ducked as she yanked herself free from his hold and threw him another punch, her fist striking his cheekbone as he raised his arm to shield his face. "Jeeze—"

"Don't tell me to grow up, Darren. I'm eighteen. I'm not a child." Ellie gasped as he gripped her by the neck of her sweater, and leaned in close.

"Throwin' yourself from a movin' car is grown up, is it? See that truck beltin' down the road?" He jabbed his finger towards the articulated vehicle disappearing into the distance. "That's where you'd be right now, under its fuckin' wheels."

Ellie elbowed him away. "Do you really care?"

"What do you think?" He sat back in his seat, flinching as he touched his cheek.

Ellie didn't know what to think, about anything. Darren had changed so much in the four years since her stepsister left him. Charlotte had turned evil that year, but even Charlotte couldn't turn a cheerful, laid-back guy like Darren into such a desperate, crime-driven man that he'd work with a deviant like Braddon.

"What's going on, Darren? Why me?" she said. "What have I done wrong?"

Darren stared ahead as Ellie tugged at the handcuffs, trying to twist her hand through, but it hurt too much, and she lowered her hands to her lap, biting her lip.

"Why do you keep handcuffs in your car?" she said.

He tested his lower jaw with a slow, side-to-side motion like a boxer recovering from a left hook. He drew breath before glancing over at the shackles.

"I don't," he said. "They're Braddon's."

"They don't look like Braddon's." Ellie paled as a strange look passed through his eyes. She looked down, tugging hard. The seatbelt and the handcuffs conspired against her, in collusion, and she couldn't escape unless Darren unlocked the handcuffs. *Shit.* She pulled and yanked, but she couldn't free either of them.

"Leave them alone," he said.

She twisted the cuffs but he glared, and she subsided. "Will Braddon come straight after me?"

"Not yet."

"Not yet?"

"I've got his car keys."

Ellie recognised the long, rusty key to the cellar door amongst the other keys on the fob, which lay on the open shelf below the dashboard, and a shiver slithered down her back.

"What will he do if he catches me?"

He put the car into gear, and then checked the mirror. "Make me stop again, and you'll find out."

He drove out of the layby, and then joined the minimal traffic heading southwest, Ellie clinging onto the door pull as he drove fast. He didn't stop anywhere for long, holding her arm tight whenever he slowed for the occasional red traffic light. Ellie sensed his apprehension as he glanced through the rear view mirror, his eyes troubled, his clenched hands gripping the wheel, and his throat moving as he swallowed hard.

Ellie thought of the harrowing appeals on TV news reports, appeals for the safe return of teenage girls, abducted, but found dead in woodland months later. The luckiest found alive, damaged and distraught, released from the prison of their captor's homes, feeling shame and guilt for reasons Ellie couldn't fathom until now, with an ache in the pit of her stomach, the shame of becoming a victim of Braddon's abuse. *He said I was asking for it because of my skin-tight jeans. Maybe I should have hidden my figure?*

The miles of silence whipped by, but Ellie had no idea where they were, not once recognising place names or villages as they raced passed in the night. He may have driven around in circles as far as Ellie knew, and it felt like it, how ill she felt, Darren's steely expression bringing a tremble to Ellie's hands and a shortness of breath to her chest. The pressure grew within her bladder, Ellie screwing up her face, squeezing her pelvic floor muscles as she held back the threatened deluge. *Please don't let me pee in his car.*

The motorway signs appeared in the distance, with bright lights encircling the junction ahead. Darren slowed the car and pulled onto an abandoned car dealership forecourt, the car bouncing up the curb, jolting Ellie's bladder. The car skirted the concrete bollards, stopping with a jerk, and then he turned off the headlights but left the engine running.

"Get out if you need a piss. I'm not stoppin' again," he said. "Don't think about runnin'. I'm not leavin' you alone, not even for a second."

Ellie's jaw dropped. "I can't do it in front of you. I hardly know you."

"Piss yourself then." He turned back to the wheel as if to drive off. "You'll be sittin' in it for hours. It's your call."

"You're so mean to me. I desperately need to pee. Let me out."

Darren pushed open his door, then sprinted around to the passenger side and untangled her, pulling her out into the cold night air, then he locked the cuffs around her wrists again, and gripped her upper arm. He bundled her into the woodland beside the abandoned building, Ellie stumbling in the long grass and nettles, her legs still weak from the drug, and her head a little woozy again.

He took a small packet of tissues from his pocket and passed one to her. "Stay where I can see you," he said.

Ellie's eyes widened. "Are you a pervert?"

He slowed to a stop. His mouth opened, and then closed again, with his brow furrowed. He gave a slight shake of the head, looking around, and then pointed to a nearby tree of reasonable girth.

"Get your backside behind that. You try to run, and I'll catch you," he said.

She groped her way behind the tree in the dark, the nettles scratching her legs, Ellie almost wetting herself in her haste to pull down her jeans, hindered by the handcuffs. She exhaled as the urine gushed out from her bladder onto the grass beneath her, her body shivering as the cold breeze blew around her naked buttocks.

Darren stepped forward mid-stream, Ellie's mouth dropping open and she called out to him. "Wait, I've not finished."

He stepped back as her endless stream splashed her boots, and she felt his impatience as he sighed. The stream of warm, yellow liquid trickled to a stop and Ellie shook out the tissue, struggling to wipe herself on such a tiny piece, not wanting to ask him for another while squatting with her legs wide open, and her knickers around her ankles. She held the sopping paper handkerchief between her thumb and finger, and dropped it in the bushes, then pulled up her jeans and knickers.

She crouched in the undergrowth. She had a chance of escape, but she didn't know if she could make it. Her trembling legs held her up, just. She didn't know if they would carry her, and she knew that he could catch her, for he looked athletic and strong. She knew that the longer she procrastinated, the shorter her chance of escape.

She drew in her breath, and she rose to her feet, unsteady and giddy, with her chest tight. *I know he'll catch me, I just know it.* She pushed her shoulders back, taking deep breaths, and then took a quick look into the shadows behind her. Nettles grew everywhere, with lengths of barbed wire entwined around them. Stacks of upturned oil drums littered the woodland, and she looked down at the handcuffs. *Oh shit. I can't run with these on, and there's nowhere to run to.* She squinted into the darkness, picking out a narrow path through to the houses beyond the wooded boundary. *What if I reach those houses, but no one opens their front door to me?* She heard Darren's step, and she fled.

Darren lunged after her, curling his arm around her throat, kicking her legs from under her, Ellie screaming, falling to her knees in the nettles that scratched her legs through her jeans. Darren tripped over her, Ellie crushed beneath him as he fell on top of her.

His hand clamped over her mouth. "You bitch. I knew you'd try somethin'."

She yanked his hand from her face and elbowed him in the chest. "Get off me, you bastard."

He scrambled up and tried to lift her, but Ellie kicked out, striking the inside of his thigh with her heel. He threw her onto the ground, and Ellie squealed, her sweater snagging on the nettles. She scrambled to her feet, Darren swinging her around to face him, with his teeth clenched, and a hard expression in his eyes.

"Try that again," he said, "and you'll wish you were back in that cellar."

He marched her to the car and opened the passenger door, motioning her towards it, but Ellie didn't move until she felt his fist in the small of her back, and he blocked her route to freedom. He pushed her down into her seat, then strapped her in, with his elbow digging into her chest, holding her down, Ellie feeling a little sick. He didn't seem to notice the door pull smacking into her elbow as he slammed the door. Even sitting still was painful for Ellie.

Darren darted around to the driver's door as Ellie raised her sweater, touching the skin around the nettle sting, with a burning sensation radiating from it, Ellie blowing on it to cool it as he sat down beside her.

"Serves you bloody right," he said.

Darren resumed the drive southwest, main roads giving way to minor roads, and then country lanes as time went on, and Ellie felt ill. The sweat pooled in the middle of her back and her breath came fast. She dabbed the sleeve of her sweater across her forehead, with her wrists still linked together, Ellie closing her eyes, groaning. Darren opened her window a fraction, from the controls beside him, and lowered the temperature control on the heater.

Ellie turned to him, with her eyes wide. "What's wrong with me?"

He shrugged but didn't look at her. "Withdrawal, I reckon."

"From the anaesthetics?" She let her breath escape. She could cope with that, whatever it felt like. "Will it go off soon?"

He shook his head. "Depends on what drug he gave you." He shrugged. "Nothin' I can do, beaut."

Darren drove on with Ellie feeling worse than she had in years. She tried to doze, but found sleep impossible, and closing her eyes served only to induce nausea, for he drove at speed on twisting country roads, and her taut seatbelt held her tight in her seat.

The car swerved sideways with a sudden lurch, Darren yelling, the headlights of the other car sliding away, vanishing into the dark. Ellie looked back. Two pairs of taillights chased each other down the road, one pair overtook the other on the brow of the hill, and then both pairs disappeared down the other side.

"What happened there?" Ellie, shaking, turned to the front as Darren regained control over the gears and slowed the car.

"Bloody bastards racin' each other, what else?" He exhaled, shaking his head. "He must have seen us before I saw him, or else he would have taken us out."

Ellie watched as he puffed out his cheeks. "Why didn't you see him?"

"I was lookin' at you."

Darren reached into his shirt pocket and pulled out a cigarette from the slim packet. He closed her window, and then he opened his own, before lighting the cigarette. His composure returned as he smoked the cigarette down to the filter, but the smell of smoke made Ellie gag.

"Take me home, Darren. I feel ill."

"You'll feel just as ill there." He increased the heat, countering the draught from the window.

"I don't want to be here. Take me home." Ellie turned the heater back down, but he knocked her hands away.

"You're stayin' right in that seat." The cigarette butt wagged up and down in time with his words until he pulled it off his bottom lip, and tossed it out of the window. "Leave the heater alone."

The windscreen wipers swept before her eyes as the light rain came down. An occasional car passed them on the country road, lighting up the cabin before plunging them back into darkness, with only the light from the dashboard shining out. The Devonshire border sign flashed by and she bit her lip. Devon was a long way from home. She sensed his gaze on her again, and she caught his alluring eyes tracking hers before he dragged his gaze away to the road.

He drove the car into another empty layby, parking so close to the hedge that Ellie's door wouldn't open, and she tensed. Darren winced as he pulled on the handbrake, and Ellie noticed the cuts on his knuckles. Darren glanced down at his hand, knocked the gear lever into neutral, and switched off the engine before switching on the interior reading light. He peered at his diver's watch, and then examined his knuckles. He sighed and stared out through the windscreen, into the dark.

"Why have we stopped?" Ellie said.

He opened the glove compartment in front of her, producing two cans of beer and a pre-packed carton of sandwiches, with the cold draught from the chiller icing her skin, cooling her down. He opened the cans and passed one to her, then took a swig from the other. He dropped the sandwich pack onto her lap. He kept his gaze steady while she prodded at the food, and she pulled a tiny piece of bread from the corner of the sandwich and tasted it. The bread tasted fresh, and she ate a little more, her stomach rumbling but she still felt sick.

"Why do you stare at me?" she said.

His eyebrow raised. "Don't you know?"

Ellie looked away and nodded. Responding to men's urges had caused trouble for her in the past year, coming close to damaging her impeccable reputation, and theirs. Especially theirs, being political figures

with close links to Doug's multi-million pound phar-
maceutical business endeavors, and his not-so-honest
investment dealings. Ellie's ambition for a career in
journalism had sparked a frenzied interest in her, especially when she turned eighteen. She felt far from
proud of her following.

She tensed as Darren moved her hair out of her
eyes. "Don't," she said.

"Don't fret, beaut. I won't hurt you," he whispered.

"No?" She moved his hand away, and he glanced
into the back of the car.

"Not if you stay put and keep quiet for me."

He reached into the back to retrieve a leather, biker-
style jacket, and his gaze never strayed from her as he
stepped out of the car, and put the jacket on.

She could just make out his silhouette outside as he
urinated against the rear wheel of the car, with the
sound diminished by the falling rain. Ellie wolfed
down the last of the food, and then Darren returned,
pulling up his fly as he approached the driver's door.
He reached in, took the near-empty can from her, and
dropped it outside, and then he sat down, shutting the
door on the fizzing mess oozing from the can on the
gravel outside.

"There's a few miles left to go. Don't piss me off
while I'm drivin' else you'll suffer," he said.

"Please take me home." Ellie pulled at the seatbelt,
and as she moved her hands to the buckle, he snatched
her hands from it.

"No. What did I just say? Ask me again, and you won't like what I'll do."

He started the car and drove into the country lane, driving so close to the hedge on Ellie's side of the road that the wing mirror scraped along the hawthorn. *He's taking no chances with me now. Shit. What can I do?* She stared down at her feet until the water sprayed up beneath the car, her heart leaping, and her body jerking.

The rain poured down again as the headlights picked out the floodwater in the country lane, with Ellie putting her trust in the man beside her. He drove well as the car ploughed on, with walls of water spraying up both sides of the car, and the rain slapping against the windscreen, with the demister on full, working hard to keep the windows clear, the noise reverberating inside her head.

The rain was endless, and the journey relentless, with Darren's mood becoming more agitated, and brooding, with every passing moment – the swearing under his breath, his scowl, and the hard stare, directed at Ellie, whenever she moved.

The car pulled up at a gate at the head of a field, overlooking a small rural Devonshire town that filled the valley below, an ill-fitting jigsaw with several missing pieces. He tugged her out of the car, the heavy rain peppering her face, cooling her skin as it ran down her neck. She watched him bowl Braddon's set of keys into the trees, and then he forced her over the gate. She squealed as she slipped off the lowest rung, and fell to her knees in the churned up mud on the other side.

"For Christ's sake." Darren climbed over the gate and hauled her upwards. "Keep on your bloody feet."

"I can't help it. I've got my wrists in these." Ellie rounded on him. "You should know what it's like. They handcuffed you when you stabbed Doug." She slipped in the mud as he manhandled her. "You don't care about either of us. You've hated Doug ever since Charlotte dumped you, and now all you want is his money. Who's behind all of this? Who's paying you to do this?"

"Shut up, Ellie." He raised his fist in warning, and Ellie drew back.

"You're so cruel. You've changed so much. Uncuff me and let me go."

Darren stepped forward. "I said shut up."

Ellie hit him in the chest with both fists, but he was too quick for her, and he threw her onto her back, straddling her, holding her shackled wrists above her head. Ellie struggled, but she couldn't move him, giving in with a sob when he put his whole weight on her.

"I warned you." He pulled out the key and uncuffed one of her wrists, his nails digging into her flesh as he held her down, and then he handcuffed himself to her. "From now on, wherever I go, you'll go. And I mean wherever. I've got a flick knife, Ellie. You hit me again, and I'll use it."

He descended the hillside with Ellie staggering beside him. Cold, wet, filthy, and tired, and now at his
mercy.

CHAPTER THREE

SANCTUM

The rain pounded the pavement, rinsing the mud from their jeans, as Ellie and Darren stood encircled within the yellow light that shone from the lamp above the door to the hair salon. Storm clouds raced overhead, blotting out the tiniest ray of hope in Ellie's sinking heart.

Darren hammered on the front door with his fist, crushing Ellie against the doorjamb with her arm pinned behind her back, and the handcuffs twisting between their wrists. Footsteps hurried towards them from behind the closed door as Darren raised his fist for the third time. He lowered his hand, then pulled Ellie away from the door, his lips finding her ear.

"Don't cause trouble, and don't speak. Remember what I said."

Ellie nodded, her scalp prickling as the light went on in the hallway, casting a warm glow through the opaque glass in the door. Darren released her arm from behind her back, Ellie clutching at her shoulder, as the door opened a fraction with a splinter of light escaping from the room beyond, a voice following it out with its owner hidden from sight.

"Who is it?"

"Wade, it's Darren. Let me in."

The light burst out as the door opened wide. A man hurried forward and ushered them into the hallway, casting a glance into the street before closing the door, and locking it. He turned around and shuffled towards them – a crumpled little man in a fawn suit, with his open shirt displaying his potbelly, his mop of grey hair fading to white at the temples, and his pale skin opaque like the glass in his own front door.

"My God, Darren, what's happened?" Wade's staring eyes widened. "Come into the salon."

He held open the connecting door, and switched on the lights, peering first at Ellie, and then down at the handcuffs as Darren led her into the salon.

Darren turned, pulling Ellie closer, eyeing Wade. "I need a car, food, money, everythin'."

"Why, what's happened?" Wade hurried into the room. "What have you done?"

Darren's eyes narrowed. "Wade, I need help, and I need sleep. I don't need questions."

Wade's jaw dropped open, his jowls shuddering. "Sleep? You can't sleep here, not now."

"Why?" Darren seized Wade's arm and shook him. "Who's here?"

Wade released himself from Darren's grip and pulled the salon door closed, lowering the window blind, and his voice. "Alistair Lloyd."

"Jeez—" Darren backed off. "Where is he?"

Ellie swallowed. *Alistair Lloyd?* She recognised the name from Doug's illicit dealings, and she edged behind Darren as he ran his hand through his wet hair, drawing breath.

"For Christ's sake," he said. "Where is he?"

Wade gestured to Darren to quieten, his hands flapping, and his eyes huge. "He's in my bedroom across the hall," he whispered. "He's been here all night. I really can't turn him out because people will see, and they'll talk to the press."

Darren pushed Ellie onto the elegant chaise longue next to the reception desk, and whispered a warning in her ear, as Wade vanished then reappeared with an armful of towels, their embroidered monograms as elegant as the boutique-style salon, with its scrollwork and gilt mirrors. Wade collected a comb on his way passed a workstation, and approached Ellie as Darren paced, Ellie's arm pulling taut. She yanked on the handcuffs, and Darren glared.

Wade pushed passed him and patted dry Ellie's long hair with a towel. "Alistair was talking about you, Darren, earlier this evening," he said. "It's strange how you've turned up out of the blue." He parted Ellie's hair with precision, smoothing a blob of leave-in conditioner onto her hair and combing it through. He draped a fresh towel around her shoulders and then turned to Darren. "Alistair makes me so jealous," he said. "He absolutely loves to hear your Aussie accent, and simply drools over your physique. He so wishes you were gay."

Darren grunted, took another towel from Wade, and rough-dried his own hair, fending him off as he came forward with the comb, Darren tweaking it from his fingers.

"I'm not here for a bloody cut and blow-dry," he said.

Wade glanced at Ellie, then watched as Darren combed his hair. "I never expected you to bring any girl here," Wade said.

Darren wiped the moisture from the comb on his jeans, and then passed the comb to Wade along with the towel. "She's not just any girl. D'you think I'd handcuff myself to any girl?"

"I don't know what you do with girls."

"Usually everythin', if they're up for it." Darren's sudden smirk lit up his face for a moment before Wade's question brought a frown to Darren's brow.

"How old is she?"

"She's legal." Darren's jaw set as Wade tilted Ellie's face towards the light. "Leave her alone."

Wade gasped, his hand flying up to his chest, Ellie shrinking back as he leaned towards her. "Have you caused those bruises, Darren?" Wade pointed a shaky finger at the cut to her forehead. "Did you do that to her?"

Darren looked away. "No."

"Then who did?" Wade put his hand to Darren's arm, but he pushed him off.

"Don't question me."

"But what about the handcuffs, and those nasty cuts to your knuckles?" Wade's insistence brought a mean look to Darren's stare.

"Didn't you hear what I just said?"

Darren towered over the diminutive man, and Wade backed away into the coat stand, sending coat hangers and aprons flying. Wade struggled to release himself from the stand, and then he stooped to retrieve the hangers from the floor, his potbelly wobbling with the effort as it hung over the trousers sitting low on his hips. Ellie rose to assist him, but Darren stopped her, with his hand on her shoulder, pushing her back down.

Wade straightened up, wheezing. "I'll only help you if you'll remove those handcuffs from that poor girl, and tell me what's going on." He replaced the hangers on the stand, and with obsessive compulsion, smoothed the aprons hanging there. "Alistair's a prominent politician, and I can't be seen to be harbouring you, whatever you've done."

Darren unlocked the handcuff from his wrist, leaving it dangling from Ellie's, and as he walked towards the door, he glared at Ellie and then beckoned to Wade.

"In the hall, now."

He propelled Wade through the door and closed it behind them, Ellie rushing to the door, and pulling at the handle, but it wouldn't turn, and she guessed that Darren held the handle in an iron grip on the other side.

She thumped the door and then turned, surveying the room from where she stood, her gaze darting, hunting. The phone was missing from its cradle on the reception desk, and Ellie guessed that Wade took it to his living quarters at the end of every busy day in the salon. She hurried over to the workstations, trying every drawer. Every sharp implement, locked away for the night, even the hairspray was on lock-down. Wade, it seemed, had a fear of theft and left nothing for Ellie to ambush Darren with on his return, despite a thorough search.

A car drove passed, and Ellie rushed to the window, yanking at the handle, hidden behind the Venetian blind, just as Darren returned. He dragged her away from the window, and forced her back down onto the chaise longue, gripping the neck of her sweater, his knee between her thighs, and the closed flick knife in his hand.

"What did I tell you outside, you little bitch?" he said.

Ellie cried out, wrenching his hand from her sweater, her whole body shaking as he pushed his hand against her mouth, suppressing her cry. The door opened, and Darren let go, pushing himself up, then slipping the knife into his pocket, glaring down at her as Wade bustled into the salon with a first-aid kit.

"Plasters for those nasty cuts on your hand," Wade said.

Darren sat next to Ellie and then took the first-aid kit from Wade, placing it between his feet while pushing Wade aside. He opened the kit, and removed the scissors, putting them out of Ellie's reach, with a glint in his eye as he threw her a glance. Wade stood so close that his shadow loomed over him and Darren pushed him out of his light, taking the hydrogen peroxide solution and the adhesive dressings from the kit. Ellie's eyes widened. *What is he doing? Is he into pain?* Darren dribbled the hydrogen peroxide onto his knuckles, gritting his teeth as the solution turned white, his cuts fizzing as his blood reacted with the solution.

"*Christ.*"

"You should have used the antiseptic wipes instead," Wade said. "They don't hurt like that. You should know that, in your profession. You need to wash that off, or else it will damage your skin."

Darren grunted and leaned forward, snapping off the top of an eyewash pod. Wade seemed to pre-empt Darren's next move and bustled to the reception desk before thrusting an empty gratuity tin beneath Darren's hand, catching the excess as Darren poured the clear liquid over his knuckles, screwing up his face.

Wade loomed again. "They're bad cuts, Darren. Who did you hit so hard?"

"Braddon." Darren swiped the towel from Ellie's shoulders, and held it against his hand, pushing Ellie's hand away as she tried to take it back.

"Braddon?" Wade shook his head. "I don't think I know him. Have you broken anything?"

"His jaw, hopefully."

Wade smiled. "No, no. I meant your hand."

"No, not yet." Darren gave Ellie a meaningful glance and taped a sticking plaster over each of his knuckles, grimacing as each piece of gauze made contact with the red raw skin. The plasters were of poor quality and Darren taped a second adhesive dressing over each one to hold the first in place. "Anythin' better than these bloody things?"

"No, they're industry standard," Wade said. "You've made a bad job of those plasters. You should have let me bandage your hand."

"Don't fuss," Darren said. "Go and get the stuff I asked for, and don't let Lloyd see her, 'cos he knows her family. They don't know we're together. And if they did, they wouldn't like it."

Wade hurried to the door with the promise of a car, money, and accommodation. He closed the door behind him with a soft click, and as his footsteps faded away, Ellie turned her eyes to Darren as he lowered his voice to a whisper.

"As soon as we leave," he said, "the handcuffs go back on, and they stay on."

Ellie shrank back against the arm of the chaise longue, increasing the distance between the two of them as Darren dropped the scissors into the first-aid kit between his feet and snapped it shut, flexing his hand.

"Wade doesn't like the handcuffs," Ellie said. "What will you do if he calls the police?"

"Why should he?" Darren pushed the medical kit aside with his foot, then leaned his arm along the back of the chaise longue, with his body turned towards her, and his knee against her leg. "Wade's a gullible bloke. He'll believe anythin' I tell him."

She flinched as he stroked her long hair, sweeping it over her shoulder, twirling a few strands around his index finger as he studied her. Ellie held her breath, eyeing him as he fingered the handcuff dangling from her wrist, tugging it, watching her with a keen look in his eye.

He glanced down at the crotch of her jeans, then at her tight sweater clinging to her breasts, his gaze shifting to her face as she drew her arms across her body in a protective hug. A dull thud came from the other side of the door, and he turned his head towards the noise.

Ellie swallowed. "What did you tell Wade?"

He gave her a sidelong glance. "Nothin' that you want to hear."

The fine hairs on her neck rose. "Doesn't he know that I'm missing?"

He stood up and walked over to the door, placing his ear to the panel. "No one knows. Braddon hasn't put the link out there."

Ellie lurched. "Then only you and Doug have seen the recordings. Doug hasn't called the police?"

"No. He's been told to keep his mouth shut."

Ellie watched as he walked over to the reception desk behind the chaise longue. He prodded one of the dressings on his knuckles as it worked loose from its position, then toyed with the telephone message pad on the desk, turning it around to read the scrawl, then turning it back again.

"Doug won't keep quiet." Ellie gripped the arm of the seat. "He'll call them. He has to."

"He won't." Darren bent towards her, resting his elbows on the sloping back of the seat, his mouth by her ear as he lowered his voice. "Would you call the police, if you were Doug Masterson?"

Ellie flinched. "I don't understand."

"Don't you? I think you do. We all know Doug's nasty little secrets. It's so easy to hold a man like Doug to ransom, 'cos he's got so much to lose – his businesses, his reputation, status, his home, and you,"—his lips touched her ear—"the gorgeous stepdaughter who he treats like his own."

Ellie felt a stab of fear in her heart, and as the rising panic tightened her chest until she couldn't breathe, Darren slapped her, snapping her out of the beginnings of a panic attack. Ellie lashed out, and as Darren raised his fist, Wade walked into the room, interrupting the moment. He stood, framed in the doorway, with a large bunch of keys in one hand and a credit card in the other. Darren walked up and took them in silence, Wade shuffling from one foot to the other.

"I can lend you the attic room if you need a few hours' sleep," Wade said, "but no longer. You'll have to leave before my first customers arrive as my ladies like an early morning blow-dry." He smiled at Ellie, then looked at Darren. "I'll show you to the attic room, and then I'll put the rest of the items you wanted in the car. I'll move the car out so you can put your own in the garage if you still have that gorgeous motor." Wade pointed to the keys, now in Darren's hand. "The other set of keys on the fob is for my holiday cottage. I'm having it renovated, so it's in a terrible mess. You can only use the ground floor." He shook his head and sighed. "I should have employed your friend, Brett. He made a beautiful job of this salon."

"What about the builders?" Darren removed his leather jacket, shaking off the rainwater onto the floor. Wade shot him a horrified glance, his gaze darting from one droplet of water on the tiles to the others.

"Don't do that, Darren." Wade took a towel from the pile and mopped the tiles with vigour. "I've laid the builders off for the winter. They won't get the trucks up there after tomorrow night, there's snow forecast, and the lane's too narrow for them to turn around as it is." Wade stood up, panting. "You'll need to re-fill the heating system as they've drained it down. You can light the fire as the chimney's lined." He took Darren's jacket and laid it across a hair-wash station to drip-dry. "Nice lads, the builders." Wade came back to the reception area. "One of them has such lovely manners, and soft brown hair – just like yours."

"Wade, the attic."

Wade closed his mouth and beckoned to them to follow him. Darren held Ellie tight around her waist as Wade led them up through the house, passed storerooms crammed with boxes on sagging shelves, then up to the next floor, passing tanning areas with spray booths until they arrived on the top floor at the head of the narrow staircase.

Wade leaned on the bedroom door to open it and walked into the room beyond, Darren ducking his head on his way through the low doorway as he led Ellie inside. Lit only by the street lamp outside, the room was bare, except for the double bed. Wade stood in silhouette in the doorway, and Darren turned.

"Go now," he said. "Turn the lights off on your way down."

Wade pulled the door closed behind him, the glow beneath the door vanishing as he turned out the light, and then clattered downstairs. Darren's shadow on the wall beside Ellie tugged open his shirt and jeans, and she turned back in time to see his muscular chest in the dimness before he scooped her up and dropped her onto the bed, throwing the duvet over her. A thin strip of light fell across the pillows from the skylight, and she felt the mattress sink a little as he lay down beside her and pulled down the blind.

She tensed as he turned towards her with his breath against her forehead. She waited for his hands to grope her, waited for him to strip her, and force his body onto hers, but he lay still, with his gaze tracking her every movement in the dim light.

"You try anythin'," he said, "and I'll knock you into next week. I need sleep, and I need you quiet. I've got the knife, and I'll use it. There are two blokes downstairs. Don't give me a reason to bring them up here."

Ellie shuddered. Wade was a sweet, harmless busybody with a wonderful eye for detail, and a natural flair for elegance, but, with a lover as persuasive and ruthless as Alistair Lloyd, Ellie guessed that Wade would do whatever Lloyd wished, regardless of its nature. Over two months had passed since Lloyd threatened Doug, and although Doug kept the details from her, Ellie was afraid of a confrontation with Lloyd.

The thought of Darren's flick knife brought a sick feeling to her gut for she remembered the knife driving into Doug's arm, four years ago, when Doug refused to relay Charlotte's whereabouts to him, just days before she gave birth to Darren's baby. Charlotte denied Darren the right to see his baby after the birth. Back then, Ellie was a little too young to understand the emotional turmoil, but, now, as an adult, she felt the gravity of the situation, and knew that Doug had many enemies, and some of those were seeking vengeance.

Darren lay there for over three quarters of an hour before his breathing slowed and his eyes closed, while Ellie battled to keep hers open. Neither Wade, nor Darren, had locked the door, and she recognised the real chance of freedom if she could just reach the street below. Ellie knew that, by first light, he would shackle her to him again, and it would be impossible to escape. She'd bided her time, behaving in the way that he'd asked, more or less, but now, with Darren asleep and Ellie un-cuffed, it may be her only chance.

She knew that even the slightest movement would wake him, with Darren on top of the duvet and Ellie beneath it. She could push him off the bed onto the floor, but she doubted her strength against his well-de-fined muscles that were visible through his open shirt, and Ellie felt reluctant to try. *If he doesn't fall—*

Darren groaned in his sleep, and as he turned away from her, Ellie slid her leg over the edge of the bed, masked by his movement. She lay still, waiting for the punch but his deep breathing resumed, and Ellie breathed again. She lay there a little longer, willing her leg to move again but, for a few crazy moments, it lay like a dead weight as she lay in a state of temporary paralysis. *For Christ's sake, Ellie, move.*

Ellie felt for the floorboards with her foot, but the bed was much higher from the floor than she'd antici-pated, and as the tip of her toes touched the threadbare carpet, she felt herself slipping. She gripped the edge of the mattress, her eyes wide, and her gasp audible. She was falling, and she couldn't stop herself. She let go of the duvet to stop its downward slide, and she hit the floor with a soft bump, aggravating her bruised hip. His heavy breathing stopped, and Ellie lay there in the darkness with her fist in her mouth. *Shit.*

Ellie never thought that the sound of a man's snore could be so welcome, and as he grunted and then turned over, Ellie felt like crying. She listened to his calm, steady, rhythmic breathing and she knew that she had to escape, now.

Ellie rose, her shadow falling across his face, and she ducked down, crouching beside the bed. Her plan of a silent escape now seemed impossible for the door stood at least fifteen feet from the bed, and the floorboards creaked beneath her, even as she balanced on her heels. She contemplated removing her boots to silence her footsteps, but she knew that there would be little chance of pulling them back on if he gave chase, and she would need them once outside. She could no longer hear the rain, though the ground outside was sodden.

She knew that the door was warped and stiff to open and that the noise would wake him, regardless of the stealth of her movements. She put her hand to her chest, feeling her bumping heart, and she knew that she must go through with her plan. If she abandoned it now and climbed onto the bed beside him, he would wake anyway.

Ellie took a breath, glanced at his sleeping face within the narrow strip of light, and then groped her way along the edge of the bed, fumbling in the darkness. She waited, at the end of the bed, with her mouth open and her eyes shut. *Come on, Ellie, you can't stop now*. She opened her eyes and blinked in the darkness, her stomach clenching, and her hand to her throat. She took a few deep breaths and then stole to the door, the floorboards creaking, and her legs craving to run in the opposite direction, her breaths quick and shallow.

She hesitated as her hand closed around the door handle. She would count to three, *no wait, five*. She listened out for his breathing, but only silence responded to her wishes. Was he listening out for her as she listened out for him? It didn't matter now that she'd reached five. She pushed down the handle and tugged hard.

The door shuddered open, and his sudden yell brought a stifled cry to her throat. She heard the squeak of the bedsprings, the floorboards creaking behind her, and the fast approaching footsteps. Her heart froze, her shoulders curling forward, and her chest caving inward. *Oh my God. Oh my God.*

His hand shot out of the darkness, clamping itself over her face, her scream bursting out of her body. His hand slid downwards, covering her mouth, with his finger sliding between her teeth. She bit hard, with the taste of antiseptic on her tongue, and Darren let go with a sudden cry of pain.

Ellie struggled through the doorway, with her heart-beat thrashing against her ribs as she staggered along the landing, her path illuminated by the scrap of moonlight shining through the roof-light above her head. She glanced over her shoulder, making out his outline in the doorway as he started after her, Darren folding with a cry as his head hit the top of the doorframe, knocking him back.

Ellie tore down the narrow attic stairway, tripping down the tiny steps in the darkness, her breath coming in gasps, her throat dry, and her lips parched. She hit the wall at the bend in the stairs and pushed herself off again, down the next flight.

Darren's warning shout from above sent someone moving far below, and as Ellie rounded the last bend in the stairs, with Darren hurtling down the stairs behind her, a figure of a semi-naked man lurched out of the shadows with another standing just behind. Wade's wide eyes loomed in front of her, with his hands outstretched to stop her. She lurched sideways, but Alistair Lloyd barred her way to the front door. She turned on her heel, and made for the back door behind her, dodging Darren's fist as it swung over the banister to catch her.

The back door swung open beneath her hands, crashing into the wall outside, Ellie tripping up in her fight to escape, falling to her knees on the wet paving outside. Her leg muscles tightened as she staggered to her feet, Ellie glancing around in the moonlight, dazed, with Darren running through the hall behind her, his breaths fast, and his footsteps heavy.

A six-foot wall enclosed the empty courtyard garden, and except for the padlocked gate, there was no way out. Ellie knew that to climb the gate was her only option, and even as she ran towards it, with pains darting through her chest, she heard Wade wheezing as he struggled in vain to keep up with the striding man behind her.

She reached the gate, pulling herself up, her triceps burning, with the rough sawn timbers scratching her hands, and the dangling handcuff scraping against the gate as she fumbled for a hold, her feet slipping off the rotting crosspieces. She dragged herself to the top and looked back, straight down into Darren's eyes. She kicked him as he grabbed her leg, splitting his eyebrow with her heel. He swore, his head jerking, with blood appearing on his skin. Ellie threw herself over the gate, falling to the ground beyond, her body shaken, hurting, then tensing as he climbed the gate.

Ellie struggled to her feet, shivering and breathless, with ice-cold sweat running down her back, and her knees bleeding through her torn jeans. She staggered onwards, passed the rear gardens of the terraced houses, then across the corner of the open field beyond, the deep wheel ruts, and water-filled ditches, jarring her legs, with the pains in her hip stabbing her with knives. He gained fast, and Ellie floundered.

The mud sucked at her boots as she scrambled up the incline towards the road, her feet sliding backwards, her thighs burning, and the mud mixing with the blood seeping from her knees. Her heart pounded, joined by the pain of exertion in the middle of her chest, and as she scrabbled for a handhold, the skin on her fingers tore on the brambles, bleeding as the thorns pierced her skin. She pulled herself upwards, towards the freedom of the road.

She heard his breath, his threats, and his anger. She could almost feel him. She struggled to swallow, her throat dry, with her screaming thighs dragging her onward. The road neared, and Ellie's whole body ached as she reached it. He reached her, and it was over.

Ellie lay where she fell with Darren squatting over her, his toned chest heaving as he breathed, with the blood oozing from a cut to his brow, running down into his eye, and a bruise appearing on his forehead. Ellie lashed out, and he caught hold of her wrist, handcuffing himself to her once more. He gripped her by the arms and jerked her to her knees.

"You're gonna hate me now," he said.

CHAPTER FOUR

CONNECTION

Mist enshrouded the crests of the brooding hills like white, swirling ectoplasm in the dwindling light of the afternoon. Deep in the valley below, near-skeletal trees overhung the bare, brown hedges. The fir trees, deep, full, and mysterious in contrast, rose up the steep hillside beyond like a triumphant army of colour, defying the onslaught of winter.

Ellie's head lolled with the motion of the car as she slept. The odour of fuel seeped into her nose as Darren pulled up at a service station, Ellie's eyes forming a blurred vision of him getting out, filling up, and then walking off. She drifted off, and then her eyes fluttered open as the car pulled up beside a cottage.

Darren kicked open his door, dashed across the garden, then scrambled over a low wall, snatching clothes from an outdoor washing line before sprinting back to the car. She heard him lift the boot lid, then felt the car shake as he slammed it closed. Darren appeared at the driver's door before throwing himself into the seat, then driving off at speed.

She slid into a dark, disturbing sleep, haunted by flashbacks that raced before her in vivid detail. Flashbacks of the night of her kidnap – the injection in her arm as she lay on the rear seat, then Ellie coming to, hours later, unable to twitch even the tiniest muscle, her mind alert, but her rag-doll body still numbed by anaesthetics.

Flashbacks of Darren driving away from the inn alone, and of Braddon, holding the hunting knife to her mouth, the jagged blade pressing against her lips as he dragged her down the cellar steps, then forced his hand inside her jeans as she lay paralysed beneath him on the floor of the cellar.

Ellie's breath came fast, her body twitching and shaking in her nightmare hell. The ringtone on Darren's mobile phone pierced her dreams, vying for a place inside her head while floating hypodermic needles stabbed her aching thighs, and disembodied mouths spat blood in her face.

She woke with an acute pain in her stomach, and as she opened her eyes, she thrust her hand over her mouth and heaved. Darren hit the brakes, steering the car onto the grass verge beside the deserted country road as Ellie tried to pull her seatbelt free. The belt pulled taut, hampering his efforts to free her, and as he slapped her hand away, he unbuckled her and pushed her out of the car. She vomited on the ground outside, and he appeared around the side of the car and held her wrist.

"Keep still, beaut. You're spreadin' it everywhere."

"What's wrong with me?" Another wave of sickness flowed into her mouth, and Darren stepped back as she vomited.

Ellie sank to her knees in the dirt, gasping as pains shot through her sore knees, with bile burning all the way to her throat, and stabbing pains surging through her kidneys with every wrench of her guts. Darren crouched with her, holding her hair back as she retched and gulped the air.

Her confusion and nausea seemed inexplicable until she realised that someone had drugged her, and as she looked at him, Ellie's palms tingled, adrenaline rippling through her muscles. She gripped the front of his shirt, and yanked him onto his knees, with the bunched material tearing in her hand, and his shirt buttons snapping in half. His eyes widened in surprise, and then he gritted his teeth as she dug her nails into his chest, leaving blood-red marks on his tanned skin, his toned chest showing through his gaping shirt.

"You let Alistair Lloyd drug me, didn't you? Didn't you?" Ellie yelled.

"Why the hell would I?" He tore himself free and backed right off as she threw up, the vomit just missing his legs.

Ellie retched again, her body aching, with the tiny blonde hairs on her arms rising as the tingling sensation crept over her body, right down to her buttocks, and she vomited again. *This isn't happening to me.*

"Don't give me that shit," she said. "I've felt this before when Braddon drugged me." She retched hard. "I was tripping in my sleep. You bastard. How could you let him do this to me?"

Darren moved in, holding her hair clear of her mouth, but she pushed him off, her long hair swinging back across her face, and she snatched it away as she gagged.

"I know it was Lloyd." Ellie's aching stomach muscles constricted, and her face burned with each surge of vomit. "I heard him speak, and I heard him say my name." She couldn't breathe as she retched, and as she gasped for air, the vomit came down her nose.

"Stop trying to breathe in. You're makin' it worse." He produced another tissue, which she snatched from his hand.

"Piss off, leave me alone."

"Bloody drown in it then." Darren walked away and leaned back against the car with his hands in his pockets, his mouth set in a hard line, and an expression of irritation in his eyes.

Ellie wiped the stinging tears from her eyes, then wiped her nose and mouth with the tissue, angry at herself for the ease at which they had duped her last night.

She remembered how drowsy she felt, sitting in the salon chair, after drinking the tea, with Wade's hands on hers, steering the cup to her lips. She had a vague recollection of Alistair Lloyd's reflection in the mirror, standing behind her chair, and then the sharp prick in the back of her hand a few moments later. She remembered hearing Wade's voice addressing Lloyd from the doorway, with the empty cup and saucer in his hand, Darren pacing near the window, and Lloyd talking with him, his reflection walking away from the mirror towards him. She remembered nothing more.

She knelt by the car while her sickness faded and she guessed, by the rapid decline of her stomach cramps, that little remained of the drug administered to her last night. The hallucinatory dreams were worse this time, the retching more violent, a different drug maybe.

She sat back, drawing her feet away from the vomit, and she rested her forehead against her knees. She recoiled and examined her knees through her torn jeans. A clear discharge seeped from the cuts from when she had fallen last night, and she wiped the wetness from her forehead with her sleeve, then pulled the sleeves of the sweater over her hands, pressing them against her knees, stopping the clear, oozing puss. The intense heat from her body dissipated as the sickness died away, and then the coolness of the winter curled around her, and she shivered.

"I saw him, Darren, through the mirror."

Darren's expression hardened as the muscles pulled taut in his cheeks, and Ellie didn't press him further. She didn't like the silence, nor the bud of fear unfurling deep within her gut.

She looked up through her tangled hair, catching sight of the phone box down the lane, a short distance from the car. Darren stood between Ellie and the phone box, and she knew that it would be impossible to keep him out while she made a distress call. A pay-phone was just that, and Ellie had no money. Whoever she rang, she knew that she would be miles away before the police arrived, with her aching body wedged into the boot of the car, and the unforgiving man at the wheel. Ellie guessed that the police would know her location at the time of the call, even if she didn't. *They'll trace my call, and they'll know I've been here.*

"Don't even think about it." Darren withdrew the closed flick knife from his pocket and opened the car door, jerking his head towards it. "Get in."

"I can't. I'll be sick."

Ellie squinted passed him, trying to guess the distance from the car to the phone box. Thirty, maybe forty yards, maybe more. She hoped that her dwindling energy would get her there.

"You won't be sick," he said. "You've finished all that shit. Get in."

"I told you, I can't."

She heaved herself up from the sitting position and crouched, awaiting her chance, but she sensed danger as he straightened. Darren's index finger hovered over the switch on the handle of the knife, and Ellie shrank back as he walked towards her.

"Get in the car."

"No." Ellie covered her face with her arms as he seized her elbow. "Darren, no."

He pulled her arms away from her face and pressed the switch on the folded knife. The serrated blade sprang from its housing and then locked into place, an ugly knife, much smaller than Braddon's, but just as cruel.

"Get in the bloody car."

Darren jerked Ellie to her feet, and as she struggled against him, he dropped the knife, which bounced, handle first, off the toe of his boot and skittered under the car. Ellie snatched the mobile phone from his shirt pocket and kicked him hard in the ribs as he crouched to retrieve the knife. He fell against the car with a cry, and Ellie stumbled down the lane, her heart thudding, and her knees so stiff and sore that she could only stagger at first. *Ellie, run, for God's sake.*

She broke into a painful sprint, pressing the emergency call icon on the phone, but nothing happened. *Oh, my God. Why won't it work? What am I doing wrong?* She tried again, then swiped her finger across the icon, and she let out a huge breath as the keypad appeared on the screen. She misdialled, time and again, Ellie whimpering, her fingers shaking so much, and her legs hurting as she ran. Her legs needed speed, and her fingers needed time, but she had neither. She entered the numbers again, checking and rechecking, then pressed the dial icon. The screen went black, and she prayed that the phone would dial out. She held the phone to her ear but heard nothing more than the blood throbbing through her ears, as she ran along the tarmac road. She doubted that her call would hold out until the end, with the signal strength dropping every second.

The shadow of the hill fell across her, and she knew it would block what little signal remained. She lowered the phone, the screen displaying the failed call message, with a cry of despair fleeing her dry lips. She re-keyed the numbers, and as she pressed the dial icon again, she heard the car start behind her, and she stumbled headlong down the lane, aiming for the woodland, the pain in her hip, and the heaviness of her limbs, throwing out her natural gait. *Don't let him catch me. Please don't let him catch me.*

The phone call connected with a sudden surge in signal strength, and as the car drew alongside her, she heard the familiar voice, a little shaky, and strained, on the receiving end of the call. Ellie sobbed with relief, but as the signal weakened again, she knew that she had little time.

"Doug, help me. He's got a knife, he's—"

She heard the car door open, then running footsteps, and as she shot a terrified glance over her shoulder, Darren brought her to the ground, with her body crashing to the floor. Darren kicked the mobile phone from her hand, forced her face into the damp earth, deadening her cries, and then he disconnected her call.

"You bitch. You absolute bitch," he said.

Ellie waited for the pain, the knife, his fists, anything. It came as a short, sharp smack across the back of her head with the palm of his hand, and as he whipped her onto her back, with his knees either side of her legs, she punched him in the ribs, Darren flinching, his mouth opening, gasping.

He grappled for her hands, with his eyes hard, and his jaw tight, gripping her wrists as she kicked his thigh, and as he let go of her arm, and slapped her, Ellie struck the side of his head with her fist, Darren reeling. She punched him again, and as he wavered, she brought her knee up into his groin, and he gripped his testes with his head down, his face draining, and his eyes creasing.

"Oh, you bitch."

Ellie tried to wriggle out from under him, but he snatched the handcuffs from his back pocket, and then forced her arm to the ground, snapping the handcuff around her wrist, and then he shackled himself to her. He seized her free arm as she lashed out at him, holding her down as Ellie slumped back with a long, drawn out breath, dazed and breathless.

She heard him panting above her, and she knew that he was hurt, and winded. She shifted, and he eyed her, poised, ready to restrain her at the slightest movement, but Ellie felt beaten. She couldn't escape now, even if she had the energy, handcuffed to him like a criminal.

She wiped the mud from her cheeks, and then turned her head away, spitting the soil from her mouth. It wasn't a pleasant sight, but she didn't care, for her dignity had vanished the moment that Braddon had snatched her.

Ellie glanced through the trees at the car, with its engine running and the driver's door open. It carried the hallmarks of a TV drama crime scene, and she looked away, her eyes welling up.

Darren sat back and opened his torn shirt, pulling it out over his jeans, studying the scratches to his chest, the bruising to his ribs, and the fiery red mark branded on his tanned skin from Ellie's boot. He winced, then exhaled.

"The next time you pull a stunt like this," he said, "I'll break your bloody neck." He adjusted the handcuffs between their wrists. "From now on you'll do what I tell you to, else I'll take you back to Wade's, and keep you drugged. It's your call."

Ellie sat up, shaken and giddy, with the taste of mud merging with the remnants of vomit. She put her head in her hands and groaned, brushing him off as he tugged her arm.

"I can't get up yet. Don't make me," she said.

"We can't stay here."

"I know, but I feel sick," she said.

"Not as sick as I feel after that call."

He lifted his arm, Ellie's lifting too, held up by the shackles, her hand as limp as the rest of her tired body. He pulled her arm and Ellie climbed to her knees, her legs shaking, and her head spinning.

"Promise me that no one will drug me again?" she said.

"That's up to you."

He stood for a moment, massaging his ribs with his eyes closed, then he pulled her up and took her weight as her knees buckled. He led her to the car as Ellie limped alongside him, the handcuff pulling tight between them. She twisted her arm, the shackle digging into his wrist, and he sucked air in through his teeth, glaring down at her.

"Do that again, and I'm headin' straight back to Wade's."

She sank into the passenger seat with a sigh, facing him as he crouched outside. Ellie let him wipe the mud from her face with a tissue, and she eyed him, seeing the pained expression on his face, with his eyes averted and his mouth downturned. *Is he sorry?* She watched him throw the tissue onto the ground.

"You don't care if the police find that?" she said.

Darren pushed himself up, grimacing. "Nah. You've left a pile of vomit for them, back up the road. I think they'll know that you've been here. If they're lookin'."

He leaned over her and un-cuffed his wrist, shackling her to the steering wheel, Ellie gaping, tugging, but the cuff held and she turned her eyes to him.

"You're not going to drive with—"

"Maybe."

He swung her legs into the car and clipped the seatbelt around her, Ellie keeping her elbow clear of the door pull as he slammed the door. She watched him with her mouth open as he walked around the car.

He sat in his seat, examined his bruises in the vanity mirror, then adjusted the adhesive plasters on his knuckles. He repositioned his diver's watch, wiping the mud from its strap, and then sighed as he looked down at his dirty jeans. Ellie caught his glance as she sat, shaking, cold, and dirty, watching him.

"Who did you call?" he said.

"Doug, but he couldn't hear me." Her lower lip quivered. "He couldn't hear a thing."

"You're sure he couldn't hear you?" Darren flinched as he shifted his position, with pain showing in his eyes.

"He didn't even know I was there. He just kept saying 'Hello', and nothing else." Ellie's body weakened, and she closed her eyes. "I had to try. You would do the same if you were held by a guy with a knife." She looked at him as he grunted. "You would, wouldn't you?" she said.

"No. I'd have picked the knife up and stabbed the bastard."

He wiped the sweat from his brow, grimacing as he caught the cut that Ellie had given him last night in Wade's backyard. He shot her a pained look, then released her from the wheel and then handcuffed her right wrist to his left.

"Are you crazy?" Ellie said. "You can't change gear like this."

He glanced at her with a glint in his eye. "Who can't?"

Ellie swallowed, with her hand trembling against his. "Oh God."

"Don't look so scared. I won't crash." He eyed her with a shrewd look in his eye. "I thought you liked being handcuffed to a fit bloke."

"What?" Ellie sat up straight. "I don't."

His eyebrow raised, the corners of his mouth twitching. "Not even . . . fluffy . . . handcuffs . . . Ellie?"

Her eyes opened wide. "What do you mean?"

He grinned, then winced, drawing breath as he held his ribs. "I watched you for a few weeks before the snatch. I reckon you know what I mean."

Ellie gulped, sliding down in her chair, with her head down. *Oh. My. God.*

"You made some sexy moves in that bloke's conservatory," he said. "Turned me on. Let's just keep that between me and you, beaut."

Ellie closed her eyes and took a deep breath, before letting the air escape, with her cheeks burning. He slipped the car into gear, Ellie's arm jerking as the car pulled away.

Darren drove fast along the narrow country road, with the winter chill flowing into the cabin through his open window. Ellie's shoulder pulled each time he changed gear, and she dragged his hand from the lever, the gears crashing. Darren resorted to driving with his fist curled tight around the lever, whether or not he changed gear. Ellie curled her fingers away from his hand as he stroked them with the back of his index finger, a knowing look in his eye.

The windows misted, and he raised the window until it closed with a soft thud, and then he flicked on the heater. The hot air blasted Ellie's face, and she turned the vent towards her window, wiping the mist off the glass with her grubby sleeve, the broken threads from her cashmere sweater hanging from her cuff.

He drove with confidence as though he knew the route, and then took a right turn into a narrow, stony track alongside a shallow stream, its banks lined with oak trees. The car pulled up onto the grass after a few hundred yards, and the engine cut out. Silence returned, except for the gentle, calming trickle of the stream, and Ellie felt intimidated by the seclusion.

He sat back with a groan, his head against the headrest, his eyes closing for a second, and then he blew out his cheeks as he clutched his ribs.

"Shit."

"I didn't think that I'd kicked you hard," Ellie said. "I had no strength."

"You bloody floored me." He turned his head. "You kicked me when I wasn't lookin'."

He released his wrist and Ellie sat still until he appeared at the other side of her door, and then lugged her outside. He shackled her wrists together.

Ellie looked up, her mouth dropping open. "I thought you were going to –"

"To what? Handcuff you to me?" His sudden, handsome grin brought a sparkle to his eyes and a flutter to Ellie's chest. "Disappointed beaut? Maybe we'll do that later, when you're cleaned up, and smellin' beautiful again." His grin vanished as he grimaced, pushing his hand inside his shirt, massaging his ribs.

He guided her to the stream, then kicked a smooth pebble into the meandering flow. The pebble clattered onto the protruding rocks, and he peered into the swirling water as it disappeared beneath the surface.

He turned. "It isn't deep. Kneel down and swill your mouth. I'll hold you."

She shrugged him off. "I can manage, thanks."

Ellie crouched on the edge of the bank and leaned forward, with her hands cupped in front of her. Her foot slid from beneath her, and as she slipped towards the stream with a cry, Darren reached out, and grabbed her, with his strong arm supporting her weight as she struggled to find her feet, and then he pulled her back onto her ass.

"Why did you say you could manage?" he said.

He crouched behind her and held her hips tight as she leaned forward. Ellie splashed ice-cold water onto her face, swilled her mouth, then dried her face with her sweater. She sat back, but he didn't let go, his hands still clasping her hips. He leaned forward, with his chest against her back, then wiped the handcuffs dry on the tail of his shirt. She caught the faint, woody scent of his aftershave as he whispered in her ear.

"We don't need to fight, beaut. I could do things for you, Ellie, believe me."

Ellie swallowed, reddening, her hands trembling. She felt herself jolt forward as he raised himself up from the ground. She looked up as he looked down, and he winked.

"I mean it, beaut."

Ellie watched as he crouched beside the stream; an attractive man in an attractive landscape – rugged and windswept. His torn shirt flapped open in the breeze as he splashed cold water onto his face and the back of his neck, the water running around to his collarbone, and then down his chest. Ellie watched the droplet of water trickle over his nipple as he dried his face on the sleeve of his shirt.

Darren stroked his chin, the designer stubble a little longer now than yesterday, maybe longer than he liked. Ellie knew that feeling, a full four weeks since her visit to the beauty rooms for her first full Brazilian bikini wax, and the brand new stubble growth in her bikini area was starting to itch.

Ellie looked up into the hazy sky, and then lowered her gaze to the low-lying mists that cut the hills in half and turned the fir trees into deep green ghosts. The moorland loomed above them with winter lurking in its shadows.

"Is Wade's cottage as secluded as this?" she said.

"Yeah, I reckon."

Oh shit. What if he tries it on? What if he comes on to me when I'm handcuffed to him?

Ellie saw the look of suspicion in his eyes as she rose to her feet and he stood up, with his hand hovering over the pocket of his jeans.

"Where you goin'?" he said.

"I'm cold. I want to go back to the car."

He gave a slight nod, then followed her, Ellie blowing out her cheeks as she limped back to the car. He opened the door and manoeuvred her into her seat.

Ellie stiffened. "Does Braddon know about Wade's cottage?"

"Doubt it. He doesn't know Wade." He handcuffed her to the steering wheel then shut the door, and stood still, with his face creased in thought.

Ellie opened the door again. "But Braddon must know Lloyd. He has to."

"I thought you were cold."

Ellie closed the door again, and then Darren wandered around to the driver's side, his brow creased and his eyes troubled. Sitting in his seat with his back to her, with one foot on the doorsill, and the other on the grass outside, Darren took a cigarette from the dwindling packet and put it to his lips.

Ellie watched as he cupped his hands around the lighter. "It's Lloyd, isn't it?" she said.

The lighter flickered before it lit the cigarette and he took a drag. He flicked the ash from the end of his cigarette, the smoke drifting from his mouth and then he stared out at the trees.

"Is what Lloyd?" he said.

"He threatened Doug," she said, "in September, but Doug wouldn't talk to me about it. He kept asking me where I was going, who I was with, and when I'd be back all the time. I just thought he was a pain, but I was wrong." She leaned towards him. "You're working for Alistair Lloyd, aren't you?"

He glanced over his shoulder, his eyes narrowing as he took the cigarette from his mouth. "If I was workin' for Lloyd," he said, "d'you think that I'd take you straight to him?"

"Yes," she said. "Because you did. Only you didn't know he was there until Wade said so. You looked shocked when you found out. And I heard you talking. I heard Lloyd say that he didn't care who'd got me as long someone had."

Darren took another drag, then threw the cigarette onto the ground outside, and stamped on it with his heel, screwing it into the grass. "If that's what you heard, I can't argue with it."

"Why is he doing this?" Ellie said. "What have I done to him?"

She shook her head, unable to think of a single reason for Lloyd to hate her so much. He wasn't a man that she knew well. She saw him on occasion when he'd appear, uninvited, late in the evening, with Doug ushering him into his study, and Ellie overhearing the ensuing rows, and the threats, the door a mere dampener for their raised voices.

"What did I do wrong?" she said.

"You've done nothin', beaut."

Darren shifted in his seat, a hand to his ribs. He leaned forward for a few seconds and then leaned back, nothing seemed to help the discomfort, and Ellie felt the brief pangs of guilt, her eyes downcast.

"But he can't be doing all of this for nothing." Ellie slumped back in her seat with a heavy sigh. "I can't think of a reason why he would do this to me."

"It's not about you."

Ellie heard his sharp intake of breath as he twisted in his seat, and she looked over at him. "Then what is it?"

She noticed a pale scar along his collarbone, maybe the result of a recent break, perhaps in the last few years. She traced the snaking line with her gaze until it disappeared beneath his shirt, towards his shoulder.

Disappointed, Ellie returned her gaze to the start of the scar and traced its visible length again.

"Doug threatened to expose Lloyd's sordid, secret life to the press," he said. "Lloyd couldn't handle that."

Darren didn't seem to notice her staring at his torso, nor mind her probing questions, and she guessed he just wouldn't answer those he found intrusive.

"Lloyd's secret life?" she said. "About being a gay politician?" She frowned. "What's bad about that?"

Ellie strained to see if he had other scars on his body, but, unless he stripped naked, she would have to settle for his collarbone. Then, with brief satisfaction, Ellie noticed the faint, vertical scar, just above the low waistband of his jeans, to the left of the sexy buckle on his belt, heading downwards. About to trace it, like the other, Ellie shrank back as he turned towards her.

"Lloyd bein' gay isn't an issue," he said. "It's his male escorts, drugs, and doin' underhanded business deals with people like Doug, that's the issue."

The breeze wafted through the car, and Darren rolled his sleeves down, leaving them open at the cuffs, the bright white fabric in the creases a marked difference to the rest of his mud-stained, grass-stained shirt.

Ellie felt her eyebrows wrinkle as she frowned. "But why has Doug threatened to expose him? I know that Doug has faults—"

"Faults? He's a connivin', robbin' bastard. Don't try that all-innocent look, beaut." He eyed her. "They hate each other. Doug made a fool out of Lloyd. He faked investments using Lloyd's money, serious money. Then he pocketed the money and blackmailed him. Now Lloyd wants revenge, and he wants to make Doug suffer."

"But he isn't suffering, is he? I am," she said.

Darren leapt as his mobile phone rang, with his shirt pocket lighting up as the rock song blasted out, and as he plucked the phone from his pocket, he glanced down at the screen. Ellie sensed his suspicion as he squinted, rejected the call, and then turned the phone off, blocking her only real chance of making calls. He stared at the blank screen, chewing the inside of his lower lip.

"Why didn't you answer that?" Ellie said.

He looked up and crammed the phone into his pocket. "Wrong number."

She held her breath. "Was it Doug ringing back?"

"No. He's not that bloody stupid."

No one receiving a misdialled call would look so uneasy. "Did Lloyd know that you were going to snatch me?"

"From Braddon? No." He looked down at his hand, smoothing the plasters around each knuckle. They didn't stick, and he snatched each plaster off and threw them into the foot well.

Ellie eyed the cuts to his knuckles as Darren flexed his hand, and she felt compelled to watch the skin splitting, and stretching over the raw skin beneath, even when it turned her stomach.

"Lloyd didn't order you to come back for me?" she said.

"No."

He picked at the broken skin. Ellie shuddered as he twisted the skin between his fingers and pulled it until it tore away, dropping the crusty flakes outside onto the grass.

"So why did you risk everything by coming back?" she said.

Darren threw her a warning look, Ellie detecting the abrupt end of their question and answer session. She looked away, her shoulders dropping and her fingers plucking a stray blonde hair from her sweater. *Maybe he's said too much already.* People felt compelled to tell her their secrets, even when she didn't want to know them. Ellie could write a book on the secrets entrusted to her.

Ellie put up her hand and knocked down the visor above her, peering into the mirror, looking for the remnants of the Ellie that everyone knew. The eighteen-year-old doppelganger, staring back, replaced the old version of Ellie, with bruises to its cheekbones, and a cut to its brow. It wore a sorrowful expression, with sunken cheeks, and tired eyes.

As she scrutinised her reflection, she scrutinised her life, the real life outside this surreal world. The life she muddled through, surrounded by businessmen and politicians, most of whom she didn't care for, some aspiring to be her sugar-daddy, and some just wanting her legs tight around their waists for an hour, or two. She spent many weekends holding them at bay, while Doug jetted off on business trips oblivious to their interest in her. She'd succumbed to a few of them, satisfying her curiosity, but their sleazy lives had left her feeling raw. Her friends thought that she had a perfect life, but they didn't know the truth, nor did they understand her need for a man in her life and an honest relationship.

Ellie thought of Darren Broderick, sitting next to her in the car, recalling his laugh, his grin, and the way he and Charlotte kissed and touched when they began dating, five years ago, almost hidden from view in the back of his car. Unbeknown to him, Ellie's secret, teenage fantasies, in which Darren featured as the dark-haired, sexy stranger, getting down and dirty with her behind Charlotte's back, were coming back to haunt her.

"D'you always stare at yourself in the mirror for so long?" Darren's sudden question, accompanied by his wide grin, brought her back to the present with a jolt and she flushed.

"No, no I don't." She knocked the visor away. "Please shut the door. I'm really cold now."

Darren slammed the door, then turned the ignition key, with the engine misfiring, threatening to stop. He frowned, jigged the accelerator, then unlocked the handcuff from the steering wheel, letting it dangle from her wrist. His grin reappeared as he faced her.

"You can loosen up, now you're with me," he said. "I can make this easy for you. Really easy. No one needs to know."

He leaned right over her and reached for her seatbelt, Ellie feeling his other arm slide around her shoulders, and as he drew the belt across her, she met his eyes. He hesitated, holding the buckle somewhere above her breast, his face keen, with his gaze dropping to her lips, and then to her cleavage. He lingered there until, with a deep breath, he tore himself away, back to the wheel, leaving Ellie alone with her thoughts. And her feelings – the sudden longing, the tiny flutter, the slight throb between her legs. As Ellie bit her lower lip and glanced across, he caught her eye and winked.

CHAPTER FIVE

DEVIANT

The towering conifers, in the plantation above, cast a long shadow across the clearing, dwarfing the cottage beneath – an unwelcoming scar disfiguring the landscape, once an obvious row of terraced dwellings, now car-crashed together into one ugly cottage, in need of euthanasia. It lay at odds with Wade's attempt to recreate a masterpiece that no one had ever painted.

Ellie bit her nails as Darren navigated the car through the narrow entrance to the clearing as they left behind the narrow country lane, with its tiny, vehicle passing-places, and deep potholes. The engine misfired and then stalled, with a dark, smoky haze enveloping the car. He let the car roll along the sloping gravel drive, and then he snatched on the handbrake, but the car continued its slow, forward motion, colliding head-on with a pile of sawn logs, jolting the car, and Ellie's nerves. He tried the ignition, but the car failed to start,

Darren calling the engine a 'bastard shit' as he strode outside.

He clambered over the logs, peering at the bumper before ducking down in front of the car, disappearing from her view for a while before he reappeared, tugging, and cussing until he straightened, with the damaged number plate in his hand. He flung the number plate into the back of the car and then rescued Ellie from the tight seat belt, tugging her outside, and then he shackled her, locking the car.

Darren slipped his arm around her shoulders and propelled her towards the cottage, guiding her around piles of rotting timbers and rusting boiler parts strewn across the yard, in front of the dilapidated out buildings, the cottage dispiriting with its bricked up, defunct entrances and mismatched windows.

The pungent odour wafted towards her, enhanced by the descending mist. Ellie held her nose, and Darren looked grim as he stopped at the bottom of the steps.

"I hope you don't have to use the dunny," he said. "It's a shit-hole. I can smell it from here. It's comin' from the gap under the door."

"What's a dunny?"

"An outside shit house—"

"You mean a toilet." Ellie wrinkled up her nose in disgust at the smell and his coarse definition. "Do you have to be so crude?"

He shrugged. "Call it what you like, beaut, it won't smell any better."

"We don't have to use it, do we?"

Ellie knew that she'd rather suffer chronic constipation than hover above a stinking pit, with a year's worth of excrement beneath her. *What if it's on the seat?* Her involuntary shiver brought a lift to the corners of Darren's mouth. He glanced down at the ground and then grinned.

"Nah, beaut, you won't need to use it," he said. "Only if you wanna piss or shit."

"Oh piss off. Don't tease me." Ellie shrugged his arm from her shoulders, and he laughed at her, with a mischievous look in his eye.

"No worries beaut." He slipped his arm around her waist. "I've found you a funnel so that you can stand up to piss like a bloke."

"You're kidding me?" She pulled back, but he held her tight.

"Nah, I mean it, beaut." His eyes shone, but his face looked serious, and Ellie believed him.

"Shit, Darren, I can't do that."

"Why not? Blokes do it all the time." He stooped, picking up a filthy, plastic funnel, cracked and slimy, and full of snails.

Ellie squealed, smacking the funnel out of his hand. It ricocheted off her leg, onto a pile of corrugated iron sheets stacked between the steps and the external cellar doors. The shuddering metal heap bounced grit, and dirt, upwards, until the whole load settled down to its usual mediocre life, a slight shift to the left of its original position, neater if anything.

Darren smirked. "Looks like it'll have to be the dunny then."

He led her up the steps and into the porch, trying several keys on the fob until he found a match for the front door, Ellie shivering beside him. He led her into the cottage, locking the door behind them, and as Ellie turned and found herself inside a huge kitchen, Darren cursed and turned to go back outside but, with a sudden change of mind, he came over to her. He un-cuffed one of her wrists, drew her to the set of drawers beside the sink, and then clamped the free shackle around the handle of the top drawer.

Ellie jerked the handcuff. "Darren, for God's sake—"

"Stay there."

Ellie rolled her eyes. *So unnecessary. Where does he think I'm going?*

Darren tried numerous keys until he unlocked the door and strode outside, with the porch door swinging, and a swagger to his stride, Ellie watching through the window as he lifted the boot lid of the car.

Ellie tugged hard at the drawer, trying to pull it out of its casing. Crammed full of old junk, it jammed on its buckled runners, and she wrenched her shoulder, a hot rod of pain drilling through her joint, spreading up to her neck and down her arm, Ellie cursing like a builder as he entered the porch.

"I can't leave you alone for a minute," he said.

His voice came first, followed by two huge boxes that he dropped onto the large farmhouse table in the middle of the kitchen, Darren groaning with the effort. He lifted one box from the top of the other, setting it down, and then leaned on it for a few seconds, cradling his ribs, and he gave her a withering glance.

Ellie ignored his unspoken accusation as she kneaded her shoulder, straining to see inside the boxes, but distance blocked her view. He uncurled with a grunt, and then locked the door, leaving the keys dangling from the lock. He returned and picked out the pile of stolen clothes from the nearest box, then looked around the room with them in his hands.

"Will you un-cuff me?" Ellie jangled the handcuffs. "You've locked the door. I can't get out."

"Maybe, if you behave for me."

He spread the clothes out over the radiator along the back wall, and Ellie wrinkled her nose, eyeing the woman's jeans and knickers, hoping that they wouldn't fit. Darren caught the knickers as they slid off the radiator, and he stuffed them up the sleeve of the sweater, next to the pair of jeans.

Ellie giggled, and then checked herself. He seemed to like her laugh, for he looked at her with his head on one side, his eyes engaging, and his mouth curving into a captivating smile. Ellie dragged her gaze from him, afraid to give away her secret thoughts.

Darren sidled over to her, his hand beneath her chin, lifting her head, with his smile lingering at the corners of his attractive mouth, his voice quiet, and his touch gentle.

"Behave for me, beaut. I'll make it worth your while."

Ellie swallowed, captivated by his soulful eyes, and his sexy smile. Her stomach fluttered, and she nodded.

Darren winked. "Good on ya, beaut."

He pushed a wooden stool towards her and then moved into the hallway, tripping over the handle of the trapdoor, protruding from the floor, on his way out of the kitchen. Ellie giggled and hoisted herself onto the stool as Darren disappeared beyond her range of vision.

She heard him explore the cottage as she nibbled on her jagged fingernail, listening to his footsteps as he ascended the stairs. His immediate descent confirmed to her that the floor above was uninhabitable and that the bathroom wasn't up there. He entered another room off the hall, and then noises thundered through the water pipes as he turned on the water supply.

Darren reappeared with splashed jeans, drying his hands on a grubby cloth that he then tossed into the kitchen sink.

"Mind that tap in the bathroom, 'cos it's a fierce bugger," he said. "There's an inside loo, you know."

Ellie watched him refill the electric boiler in the kitchen before he switched on the heating, the distinct smell of heated dust spreading throughout the cottage, Ellie longing for a warm by an open fire.

She salivated when Darren opened a packet of bacon from the box on the table and lit the grill with his cigarette lighter. He noticed her watching, and when he released her from the drawer handle, Ellie came straight to the table, dragging the stool along with her. She perched, watching him drop slices of bacon, and sausages, into the grill pan, her stomach rumbling.

Her eyebrows lifted with surprise as he cracked the eggs against the side of the cooker, then dropped the whole lot into a frying pan before fishing out the shells, burning his fingers as the hot fat spat at him. He dug out a long-handled bread knife from the drawer, then cut thick slices from the farmhouse loaf that he produced from the box. Ellie took a piece, breathing in its fresh-baked aroma. *Bless Mister Wade, whatever his first name is.*

Fifteen minutes later, they sat opposite each other, eating the hot sandwiches in silence, eyeing one another, Ellie with suspicion, and Darren with a smirk. Both had a bruise to their brow caused by each other. Ellie picked off the bacon fat and put it on the side of her plate, wiping her greasy fingers on a piece of kitchen paper as Darren sucked his. His smirk grew into a grin.

"You're a dainty little bugger," he said.

Ellie shrugged, dabbed the corner of her mouth, then offered him a fresh piece of kitchen paper. *If he's going to manhandle me, he could at least wipe his greasy fingers.*

The meal ended, and Darren leaned forward, picking up the handcuffs. Ellie put down her mug of tea, her face falling as he rose to his feet.

"Darren, don't." She slid from the stool and backed away. "I said I'd behave and I have."

"Yeah, I know. I just need to shower. It won't take long."

He opened the handcuffs, then beckoned to her, Ellie thrusting her hands behind her back, shaking her head as he straightened. He reached out, then gripped her shoulder, Ellie gasping as he spun her around, snapping the handcuff around her wrist.

He marched her through the hall, and into the tiny lounge at the rear of the cottage, hurling the dustsheets onto the floor, and forcing her onto the tattered sofa, pushing her back down when she attempted to stand. He dragged a small table towards her, then shackled her to the table leg.

"Oh, you bastard." She yanked the table over, but the cuff stopped against the horizontal stay, and she found it impossible to free it, the bolted legs refusing to budge. If Ellie wanted to escape, the table wouldn't be far behind.

He glared, set the table straight, then slipped off his diver's watch, and tossed it onto the top. "Knock it over again, and I'll lock you in the dunny."

Ellie kicked out at the table, watching as it teetered on two legs until it fell, pulling her arm, his watch striking the floorboards with a thud. She stared back at him, with her chin jutting out in defiance.

"You handcuffed me. After you said that you wouldn't."

"Ellie, I know what I said, but I'm not chasin' you outside without my strides on."

He stalked across the narrow hallway into the bathroom, leaving the doors open on his way through, Ellie leaning back with a deep sigh, watching him search the bathroom cabinet, and then the boxes in the kitchen. He headed back to the bathroom, throwing her a furtive glance as he carried a small stack of towels under his arm, with an assortment of toiletries in his hands.

He disappeared behind the open door, and Ellie tried to un-cuff her wrist, but succeeded, only, in hurting herself. Her involuntary cry brought Darren to the doorway in his tight, designer trunks, with his jeans in his hand, and a rolled up towel around his bare neck. He laughed when he saw her, and then retreated, a flush creeping over Ellie's cheeks as she watched him remove his trunks. He winked at her and then ran the shower.

Ellie sat for over a quarter of an hour until the water ceased hammering down, onto the plastic shower tray, like a tropical storm, before it gurgled away with a satisfying, guttural burp. The full-length mirror misted over, with Darren unable to keep an eye on her, and Ellie no longer able to see his full-length reflection.

He appeared in the doorway a few minutes later, with his jeans wide open, and his leather belt hanging loose, with his ripped shirt and crumpled trunks in one hand, and his boots hanging from the other. He walked right up to her, tossing his shirt and trunks onto the sofa beside her, and then let his boots fall to the floor.

She saw his scar snaking downwards inside his open jeans, longer now, disappearing into the dark hair just visible within the V-shaped opening of his fly, just above his concealed shaft.

"I've left the bath runnin' for you," he said. "It's OK. It's clean."

Ellie averted her eyes from the intriguing dark hair, level with her forehead, as he freed her from the shackles and rubbed her wrist to stop the cramp. Ellie kept her head down, for the gentle touch of his fingers sent a hot tingle through her body. She didn't want to feel the throb in her knickers, not again, not for him. *Please, not for him.* Pleading failed her and Ellie crossed her legs, tight.

She looked up, clearing her throat. "You'll let me close the bathroom door?"

"Yeah." He lifted her hands, inspecting the slight welts on her wrists, the fading nettle stings on her fingers, and her broken fingernails. "I'll lock you in there before I go."

Ellie felt her cheeks burning at his touch. "You're leaving?"

He let her go. "I'm not quittin' if that's what you're thinkin'. You're not that lucky."

He forced the handcuffs into his back pocket, and then closed the fly of his jeans. He took her hand, then led her into the bathroom, Ellie wrinkling up her nose, squinting, trying to understand, as he closed the door behind them.

"You trust me to stay here, without you?" she said.

A subtle change washed over his face as he closed the door and turned, with a shrewd expression materialising in his eyes. "You won't wanna leave."

"What do you mean?" Ellie eyed him, her arousal evaporating like a shadow in a floodlit room, with the tiny hairs rising all over her body.

He came forward, with his hand on her wrist, and a sly gleam in his eye. "I'm takin' your clothes with me."

"You're what?" Ellie shrank back. "You can't do that."

He held her arm as he turned off the bath taps, and then he faced her. "Take them off, beaut. Now."

"In front of you?" Ellie faltered as he squared his shoulders. "What have I done to deserve this?"

"No questions. Just do it."

Ellie felt cornered as he leaned back against the door. The bathroom didn't have a window, and Ellie didn't have a choice. She didn't want him to pull the knife on her, but she guessed that he might. Ellie stood still, her mind racing as fast as her heartbeat.

"I can't," she said.

"D'you want me to take them off you?" He stepped forward. "No. I didn't think you would," he said as she shied away.

"Don't do this to me. It's so unfair." Ellie's gaze darted from shelf to shelf, but nothing came to her aid.

"Life's unfair. Either you take them off, or I will."

"Promise me that you won't touch me if I do?" She backed into the side of the shower cubicle as he slipped his hand inside his pocket, her long hair sticking to the wet glass. "Say it," she said. "Say I promise."

"For Christ's sake, Ellie, just do it."

Her hands trembled as she turned away from him, slipped off her boots, and then peeled off her frayed sweater, throwing it behind her. She opened her jeans, but couldn't bring herself to pull them down. She half turned as Darren walked up behind her.

"And the rest, beaut."

She closed her eyes and drew her torn jeans down her legs, struggling to step out of them for they were tight, yanking them over her ankles, her socks coming with them, and she left the jeans where they fell.

She shivered, folding her arms tight around her middle, and then she heard him switch on the heated towel rail behind her. She opened her eyes as she felt his warm hand against the small of her back, Darren standing beside her, waiting, with his eyebrows raised, and a half smile on his lips. Ellie held her head up high as she slipped off her tiny, pretty knickers, and dropped them onto the floor.

He held her steady as she lifted her leg over the edge of the high-sided bath, Ellie well-aware of her breasts bouncing, with her smooth 'Brazilian' on full display, lips and all. She lifted her other leg over the side, and then lowered herself into the hot water, with the steam already tousling her long hair. She sank lower, leaning back as her whole body sighed with the strain of the past few days, with the tears welling up, and Ellie biting them back.

He crouched beside the bath, his sly expression melting away as his gaze rested between her legs, before travelling to her breasts, and then to her eyes. It darted from her eyes to her groin, then back again in the same compulsive way that Ellie had eyed his, earlier. He trailed his fingers in the water, with a hungry look in his eyes, his lips parting.

She covered her nipples with her arm and slipped her hand over her crotch. "Please stop staring at my bits."

A brief look of disappointment passed through Darren's eyes, and then he grinned at her. "You checked me out a few times yourself this arvo, beaut." He winked. "Just returnin' the favour."

Ellie gaped, feeling her face and neck turn scarlet. *Oh. My. God. He saw me.*

"We don't have to keep fightin'," he said. "You wouldn't get hurt and upset, and we could get through all of this." He reached for the soap. "I could make our time together really easy, you know?"

He held out the soap to her, and as she took it from him, she gave a start, her arm flattening her breasts. *He made me reveal my nipples, the dirty bastard.* Ellie looked into his puppy-dog brown eyes as he eyed her up. *Oh shit. How long can I resist him?*

"You did that on purpose," she said.

He gave her that handsome, winning smile. "Who wouldn't, beaut?"

Mesmorised, she blinked and looked away, feeling her nipples harden. "How long do I have to stay with you?"

"Until I get the call. Lloyd wants Doug to suffer."

Ellie rested her head against the tiled wall, just above the bath, and eyed him. "Don't you think I've suffered enough?"

"I won't let Braddon hurt you again."

"Braddon?" Ellie jerked upright, the water surging along the length of the bath, splashing over the taps at the opposite end. "He won't come here, will he?"

The water rushed back, slopping over the side as Darren retreated. He fidgeted with a loose thread on the waistband of his jeans, and she gripped his wrist with her wet hand, searching his eyes.

"I thought I was safe from him," she said. "You said so."

He released her hand from his wrist. "The only way he'd know where you are is if Lloyd tells him."

Ellie's eyes widened, and she clutched his arm. "Braddon will go looking for Lloyd. He'll beat Wade into telling him where I am, and he'll come after me. You know he will."

He crouched beside the bath. "Beaut, Braddon's still holed up in Salisbury. I took his keys. I told you."

"The keys to his pickup truck?"

"What pickup truck?"

"Darren, there were two vehicles parked at the inn when we came out, a car and a—"

"Christ." Darren jerked to his feet and raked his fingers through his hair. "Why didn't you tell me?"

"I didn't think I needed to." Ellie heard the pitch in her voice rise as fear gripped her. "I thought you knew."

"Shit. I need to find a phone signal. I'll be back as soon as I can."

Darren picked up her clothes, bundled them under his arm, and gave her one last, lingering look before he walked out, locking the bathroom door behind him, his footsteps striding away. Minutes later, the front door banged, and after numerous attempts, the car started. It growled away down the hill, and Ellie felt the loneliness creep up on her.

She picked up the soap, and created a lather, soaping her wet skin with gentle circular movements, for there were few places that didn't hurt. She rinsed off the soap with a face flannel, then sunk lower, with the water covering her shoulders.

She lay, staring at the ceiling, thinking of Darren driving fast in the thick, descending fog, the man tense, and determined. Of Doug, at home, unable to alert the police, powerless, and overawed. Of Braddon, with his hands around Wade's podgy throat, squeezing, and then pounding him to the floor, Wade squirming and bleeding, Lloyd slinking away. Ellie shuddered.

She closed her eyes, remembering Darren's sexy grin, the touch of his hand, and the way he gave her the eye. His intentions were clear. Ellie knew that the second she succumbed to him, he would waste no time in bending her over the kitchen table.

She lifted the chain, then pulled up the plug, the water gurgling away, Ellie sitting until the bath was empty, with a soapy film on her legs. She rose, shivering, and as she walked to the sink, she peered into the mirror to inspect her new semi-permanent eyeliner and whitened teeth. She gasped when she saw the cuts, the bruises, and the shocked face of the doppelganger gaping back at her. It wasn't Ellie. She wouldn't let it be Ellie. She pushed the fear, and the pain, onto the girl in the mirror, and looked away.

She cleaned her teeth, and then stepped into the shower, pulling the switch, then turning the dial. She lurched away from the scalding water, and snatched the dial around, with her arm outstretched, dodging the steaming cascade. *Bloody hell, Darren. How hot did you have this?*

Ellie gasped as the icy water pounded her skin, with goosebumps rising on her body, and the shiver rippling down her back and along her arms. Ellie swivelled the dial, settling for tepid. She washed her hair, rinsing away the mud, blood, and her dark memories. Her tears fell, masked by the fast-flowing water. The last of the suds drained away, and she switched off the shower, stepping out of the cubicle, then towel drying her hair as she hovered near the heated towel rail, avoiding eye contact with the girl in the mirror.

Ellie heard the growl of an unknown vehicle pull up outside, and she straightened with a frown. She stole to the bathroom door, placing her ear against it, listening out for Darren's cough, and the rattle of his keys. Ellie drew back as the front door opened, with her hand to her thumping heart, as familiar, heavy footsteps marched through the kitchen, doors banging open along the hallway, the search closing in on her, Ellie clutching her chest, afraid to breathe.

The bathroom door handle turned, the door shook, but the lock held, Ellie's hands clamping over her mouth to silence her fast, shallow breaths. The handle returned to its resting position, then nothing. Ellie let her breath escape her lips, her head falling forward as her shoulders relaxed.

The military boot smashed through the lower panel, the door splintering, Ellie screaming, cowering against the shower cubicle, the corroded door hinges bending, warping, then another crash, the lock shearing, the door bursting open, with splinters of wood striking her.

Braddon strode in, then slammed his boot into her thigh, his glare penetrating deep within her soul, with the entire whites of his eyes visible around each dark iris, and each pupil a pinprick of black.

He dragged her to her feet, then struck her across the mouth with the back of his hand. "Shut the fuck up, you dirty little slag."

He pushed his hands around her throat, squeezing, her screams dying away. She fell back against the ceramic sink, choking, her body shaking and her chest constricting as terror gripped her and paralysed her.

Her lips formed the words, but the crushing sensation took her voice. "Please don't hurt me."

He released her throat, and laughed in her face, his eyes dead, staring. His left eyelid closed in a slow blink, the right eye staring through her. "You're out of luck, Ell—"

"Let me go, please let me go. Where's Darren? Where is he?"

"I passed that bastard on the way here," he said. "I tried to run him off the road, but the fucker got away."

He raised his hand to her breast, pinching her nipple, twisting it, watching for the pain in her eyes as his tongue wetted his lips. He increased the pressure between his thumb and finger, the stinging sensation spreading through her breast, her stomach tightening, and her hands clenching. He forced his leg between her thighs, crushing her against the sink with his solid frame.

"Darren's face drained when he saw me, Ell," he said. "Shame he can't turn that long car around 'til he reaches the main road. He's shit-scared. You know why?" His mouth broke into a vile grin, with his thin lips peeling back to reveal his yellowing teeth, and his breath repulsive. "He knows I'm going to cave your head in, and fuck you as you die."

Ellie felt a stab of pain in her chest as though he'd reached into her ribcage and gripped her heart, squeezing, twisting, with his glare boring into her. She felt her urethra open, then the warm urine spraying between her legs onto his trousers. It kept coming, and Ellie clutched at herself in horror, trying to stem the flow, but it spurted through her fingers, spraying over his crotch.

Braddon looked down at her groin and recoiled, a choking noise emitting from within his throat. He snatched the damp towel from over the edge of the bath, forcing it between her legs, with the liquid dribbling over the towel, and then running inside the sleeve of his sweater.

"You dirty little bitch," he said. "How many times have I told you not to piss in front of me?"

"I can't help it. I can't help it."

Her flow dribbled to a stop, and he slapped her face, throwing the soaked towel into the bath.

"You're a mental bitch." He gripped her hair, jerking her head towards him, with his lip curled. "You left me for Darren, you filthy whore. I'll kill him, Ell. I'll hunt him down, and dismember the bastard. Then I'll rip your fucking throat out."

Ellie choked. "You're an evil, evil bastard."

She screamed as Braddon slammed her head against the tiles, with the cold basin digging into her back. He forced his tongue inside her mouth, with his saliva dribbling onto her tongue, Ellie gagging as his hard, invasive organ licked the roof of her mouth.

She reached behind her back, feeling for the space between the taps, her chest hurting with every heartbeat, and her breathing fast. She felt the cold ceramic beneath her fingers, soap-scum under her broken nails, with her knuckles scraping on the limescale-encrusted taps. *Where the hell is it? Where is it?*

She felt his tongue darting around her mouth, felt the pain in her nipples, with his fingers pinching hard. She reached behind her with her other hand, groping, feeling, her heart hammering, sweat beads running down her cleavage, running down her back. *Oh God, it isn't there. It isn't there.*

Her hand enclosed the tooth-glass, her gasp of relief audible. Shaking, and sobbing, Ellie drew the glass towards her as his tongue forced itself beneath hers, Ellie gagging, swallowing his saliva. She clutched the glass, afraid that it would slip from her grasp, the condensation trickling onto her fingers. She closed her eyes, tensing her jaw, the muscles in her arm pulling taut.

The thick base of the glass slammed against his cheekbone, but the glass didn't break. His head jerked back, but he came back at her, forcing his tongue further into her mouth, his hand crawling over her stomach, over her abdomen, and then between her legs. Ellie's whole body shuddered, with the tight knot of anger spreading through her entire being, and her muscles primed.

She smashed the glass into his forehead, showering him in shards, his skin splitting, inches from her eyes, his blood spraying along her arm and over his face. His skin drained to a tombstone grey, and he staggered back, his eyes creased, and his jaw clenched as he cradled his head. The shards fell around her, onto her shoulders, and onto the floor, splashing into the urine around her bare feet. She stole through the broken glass, her eyes wide, Ellie gasping as she slipped in the urine.

She hauled herself through the doorway, Braddon hurling himself at her, gripping her hair, kicking the back of her legs, and bringing her to her knees outside the bathroom door. He pulled her onto her back, with his arm around her throat as he tugged at the zip of his fly. She wrenched herself out of his lethal embrace, Braddon scrambling to his feet, snarling, clutching at her as she tore away, screaming.

She ran in blind panic through the kitchen, crying out in pain as her hip struck the corner of the table. She fell against the cupboards as the table juddered along the tiled floor, the bread knife rocking on its bolster on the tabletop where Darren had left it. She lost time, dragging herself up, sobbing, her breaths harsh, and her heart thrashing in her chest.

She ran for the porch, dragging open the front door, just as Braddon reached her. She felt his weight against her back, and she fell down the steps outside with him on top of her, a few feet from his black pickup truck.

Ellie's cries died into silence as he held the bread knife against her throat, with the tip of the blade nicking the skin of her neck, bringing a piercing jab of horror to her chest. He heaved her up the steps, pulling her backwards into the kitchen.

He marched her into the lounge, slamming the door, his guttural roar drowning out her cries as he fended off her beating hands, his muscles straining in his corded neck.

Her bile rose, and her chest heaved, and as she dug her jagged nails into his neck, he gave a yell, threw her off, and hit her. She fell against the bookcase, her body falling with it as it crashed against the fireplace, and he kicked her legs from underneath her, crowding her to the floor as he squeezed her throat, quelling her ability to fight. The blood pulsated inside her ears, terror gripping and clawing inside her as he held her down with his body. Braddon fumbled with the fly of his urine soaked trousers, and as he pulled his trousers down to his thighs, Ellie felt his hard, wet erection between her legs.

A car skidded to a halt outside, with the sound of gravel spraying up, and brakes squealing, then came the sound of running footsteps, tearing through the porch, the kitchen, and into the hallway. Darren Broderick wrenched open the lounge door, his eyes hard as he dragged Braddon from her.

Braddon's head snapped back as Darren's curled fist met his snarling face with a sharp crack, blood spattering onto Darren's torn shirt. Braddon careered backwards onto the floor, silent, bleeding, motionless, the knife clattering alongside him. Darren kicked the knife under the sofa, pushed Braddon's head to one side with his foot, and then crouched, with his knee on Braddon's jaw, feeling for a pulse in his neck with his fingers.

Ellie's chest heaved, her vision blurred through her tears, a tiny line of blood trickling down her neck onto her fingers as she lay, shaking, holding her other hand out towards him. Darren rose, lifted Ellie to her feet, then put her aside, and gripped Braddon's legs.

"Ellie, he's out cold. We need to get him outside before he comes to. Help me, beaut." Darren jerked his head towards the door. "Hold the doors open for me."

Ellie backed away, retching. "I don't want to touch him. Please don't make me."

"I won't make you touch him. Come on, beaut, help me."

Darren dragged Braddon's unconscious body through the hallway, and into the kitchen, Ellie sobbing, holding each door open, with her other hand to her neck to stem the bleeding. She shrank back as he dragged Braddon passed her, Darren tugging and pulling as Braddon's limp arm caught around the table leg. Ellie kicked his arm free, then scuttled back behind the door as Darren hauled him into the porch. He came to a halt at the top of the steps, panting, and then looked over his shoulder at her.

"Stay inside, darl'. I can manage now."

Ellie watched from the kitchen window as Darren rolled Braddon's limp body down the steps outside, and then dragged him, face down, across the courtyard, with Braddon's face and genitals scraping along the ground.

Darren heaved the unconscious man into the outhouse, rolling him over, and then pushing him up against the toilet bowl, with Ellie stretching to see. Braddon's body jerked as Darren's boot met his face, and Ellie shuddered, nauseous.

Darren locked the toilet door, pushed the key into his pocket, and returned to the cottage, his expression grim. He wiped the blood from the sole of his boot on the doormat, then stripped off his torn, bloodied shirt, and hurled it to the floor.

"That dunny won't hold him once he comes to," he said. "The lock's shit. I'll have to think of somethin' else." Darren wrapped his arms around her, and held her close, with his bare chest against her breasts, the warmth of his soft skin calming her. "You did some damage to his forehead, beaut, pity it wasn't his jugular."

"He's stoned, and I couldn't stop him." She wiped her eyes, his neck warm against her cheek, and his belt buckle cold against her navel. "I tried, but he kept coming back at me." She looked up at him, her lip trembling. "Will you stop him? When he comes to?"

He glanced down at her bruised, naked body, and his mouth set in a hard line, with an expression of determination in his eyes. "You can bet your life on it."

CHAPTER SIX

BLADE

Snowflakes swirled out of the darkening sky as Ellie stood transfixed at the kitchen window, watching Darren slam the car bonnet down and storm back towards the cottage, his hands in the pockets of his jeans, with his stolen sweater pulling tight across his firm chest, his jaw clenched, and his shoulders hunched.

Ellie pulled the sleeves of her sweater down over her cold hands, her knees chilled through the holes in her jeans as Darren brought the icy blast into the kitchen with him, stamping the snow from the treads of his biker boots, and then slamming the door behind him.

"Bastard car won't start." He threw the keys and mobile phone onto the table, watching as they slid across it, the keys bunching up against the side of the box as they came to an abrupt halt. "I filled up with the wrong bloody fuel at the servo, while you were out cold. Unless I can get the keys to his truck, we're screwed."

Ellie's blood iced over, and a lump, the size of a bullet, formed in her throat. *What if Braddon's conscious? What if he's lying in wait?* Ellie stood with her back to the window, rigid at the thought of Braddon, locked in the outhouse behind her, his body coiled, and primed for attack. *What if Wade's dead?* The silence crept around her like an unseen entity, like the chill in the air. *What if I'm next?*

Darren leaned back against the radiator, his gaze fixed on the floor, his hands, reddened from the cold outside, tucked under his armpits. Ellie studied him, recounting his genuine apology for leaving her alone in the cottage, and his admission of guilt for leaving the front door unlocked, in his haste to find a mobile signal, leaving her at Braddon's mercy.

Darren raised his head, a shrewd expression creeping into his eyes. He glanced passed her, through the window, and then turned his eyes to her.

"D'you think you can inject the bastard if I hold him down?"

Ellie gasped, her skin prickling. "No. No, I can't do that. I hate needles, and I don't want to touch him. I just can't do it."

He considered her for a moment, stroking his temple with his finger, before he prized himself from the radiator, and sifted through the boxes on the table, drawing out a small, plastic storage box with a sealed lid.

"I need to get Braddon's keys. They're not in the truck, and it's locked." He eased open the lid of the box. "I don't know if he's armed, I didn't check."

Ellie gasped as he took out a syringe, with its capped needle attached, and a vial. "Where did you get those?" she said.

"Lloyd." He removed the cap from the vial, revealing its rubber stopper. "It was meant for you." He raised the syringe with the needle pointing upwards, slipped off the cap, and pulled the plunger down. "It won't keep him down for long, half an hour maybe. It'll only stall him. Enough to get his keys, and then steal his truck."

Ellie swayed at the sight of the exposed needle, with her hand to her throat, and her muscles rigid. She watched as he pointed the syringe downwards and pushed the needle into the vial, pressing the plunger down. Ellie felt the colour drain from her cheeks as he upended the whole apparatus, pulling the plunger until the solution entered the syringe. A flick on the side, a slight push on the plunger, then he removed the empty vial and dropped it into the container.

Ellie swallowed, and gulped, struggling to clear her throat. "Where did you learn to do that?"

"Trained as an animal doctor." He took the flick knife from his pocket and beckoned to her. "Open the door for me and then stay here. If he charges me, lock the door, even if I'm outside. Don't let him in."

"What if you can't inject him? He's not a defence- less animal on an operating table. He's a sadistic bastard." Ellie gripped his arm. "He shoots animals, Darren. He said that he keeps guns in his truck. What if he's armed? What if he killed Wade? And what if he kills you?"

"Trust me, beaut." He draped his arm around her neck, the syringe pointing away from her. He gave her a squeeze, dropped a kiss on her forehead, and then let her go, gesturing towards the door. "Don't forget to lock it."

Ellie opened the door and retreated as he released the blade of the knife from its casing. He gripped the handle, took a deep breath, then exhaled as he passed her, walking out onto the thin layer of snow as the flakes died away, the clouds patchy, the late afternoon light fading, and the fallen snow already freezing. The icy draught blew around her, through the open door, as she watched him stride away, snow crunching beneath his feet.

Ellie walked through the porch and stood, shiver- ing, on the top step, with her arms folded for warmth, her body tingling with excitement from the memory of his touch, and an acute ball of fear edging into her gut as Darren headed for Braddon's crude prison cell.

He picked his way across the debris-strewn court- yard, the overpowering stench from the outhouse churning Ellie's stomach as she stood at the top of the steps, and as Darren glanced over his shoulder and saw her, he motioned her indoors. Ellie stood still, shaking her head, a sense of foreboding creeping up on her, a chill encasing her veins, and a quiver in her stomach as he turned away from her and moved towards the outhouse.

Darren stepped over an object in the snow, and as he put his weight back down on his foot, his heel slipped from under him, and he hit the ground with a sickening cry. Ellie screamed as the knife twisted in his hand beneath him, the serrated blade slicing into his flesh, with blood spattering onto the fresh snow. The syringe rolled away with odd, bouncing movements as the oval shaped base of the plunger jerked across the debris.

Ellie gasped, slithering down the steps as she ran towards him, her fashion boots sliding on the frozen snow, Ellie tripping over the half-buried debris in her haste, jolting her legs, with wisps of snow blowing into her face. She put her hand out to stop herself falling, and she slowed, her hand on her chest as Darren lay face down, with his forehead resting on his arm, and his body heaving as he breathed.

Ellie edged towards him, her stomach knotting as she imagined the knife embedded within his guts, his blood leaking, and his bloodied entrails slipping out of his abdomen. Darren pushed the knife away as Ellie fell to her knees in the snow, kneeling in front of him, recoiling at the sight of the blood on his hands.

His face creased with pain as he raised himself up onto his elbow, pulling at his torn sweater, and as he raised the hem, the blood welled up and ran down to his jeans. He placed his hand over the wound, with his teeth clenched, and his head down.

Ellie clutched at him, her heart racing. "How far did the knife go in? How bad is it? Did you fall on the needle? For Christ's sake, Darren, say something. You're scaring me."

She pulled his arm, and as he raised his eyes to her, a droplet of water dripped onto his cheek from his wet hair, then ran down to his jaw. His blood seeped through his fingers as he gripped the wound in his side.

Ellie's voice rose as her larynx tightened. "Darren?"

"I'm OK." His clenched his jaw as he shifted. "I've had worse."

"Let me see." Ellie pulled his hand from the wound, and the blood oozed out through the tear in his skin. She knew he felt as sick as she did. It showed in his eyes. "Oh God, Darren. You need stitches. That gash is an inch long."

He pulled his hand from hers and heaved himself onto his knees, his jeans wet, and his breathing shallow, with his hand pressing down on the wound.

"I'll be OK. Don't fuss," he said.

Ellie cast a quick glance over her shoulder towards Braddon's cell. The door remained closed with Braddon's arm lying outstretched within the gap beneath it, blood and excrement congealing underneath his jagged nails. She turned back, gagging, feeling lightheaded. She pushed herself up from the snow, her hands trembling, and the knees of her jeans soaked.

"I need to get help for you," she said.

Darren caught her elbow. "No. I can't let you do that. I'll deal with it."

"No, you need help." Ellie shook her head. "Look at you. You're in a state." She took his arm and pushed him down as he tried to rise.

He pushed her away, and then struggled to his feet, but his knee crumpled beneath him, and he staggered, gripping her arm. "*Shit.*"

She clutched at him. "Did you cut your leg too?"

"No. I fell on all that junk." Darren waved his hand over the snow-covered debris, with a break in his voice as he jerked his head towards the cottage. "I just need to get inside." He wavered, and she gripped him.

"I can't lug you back to the cottage on my own," she said.

"Ellie, I'll get there. It's not that bad." He gestured towards the knife. "Pick it up, beaut. Don't leave that out here for him."

Ellie reached for the bloodstained knife and held it out to him at arm's length, the handle dangling between her thumb and index finger, with a drop of blood dripping onto the trampled snow from the tip of the blade. He closed the knife against his thigh, returning it to his pocket, his other hand covering his wound.

He glanced at the ground, with his eyes searching, and his mouth downturned. "Did you see where the syringe landed?"

"No. It bounced over there." Ellie pointed to the left, peering at the ground. "I thought you were badly hurt so I didn't look."

"Leave it for now. Beaut, I'll find it later."

Ellie came forward, and Darren slung his arm around her neck, with his knee bent, and his face ashen. She staggered under his weight, and he winced as he straightened his leg, reducing the burden.

"I'm a lucky bastard," he said. "It's only a flesh wound. I thought for a second that I'd disemboweled myself. Somethin' shifted under my foot, and down I went. It's not so bad now. My knee's the painful bugger."

Ellie glanced over at Braddon's arm, lying on top of the snow, beneath the door. She imagined a gun hidden inside his jacket, a knife glinting in his hand, and his evil stare, Ellie with the knife to her throat, and his other hand inside her clothes. She shivered and screwed up her eyes, fighting off the images as her mind flicked through every scenario possible.

"Shit. This is bleedin' too much," Darren said.

The sound of his voice pierced her thoughts, and she returned to the present, with a deep breath and a tight feeling in her chest. She thought she saw him retch, but he made a quick recovery.

"We have to get you indoors," she said. "Don't just lean on me. You'll have to help me."

He flinched as he tested his knee. "Jeeze."

Ellie curled her arm around his waist, feeling his muscles tighten beneath her hand. She supported him with her hand to his chest, his nipple hard against her palm, and he turned his sorrowful eyes towards her.

"Thanks, beaut."

"What's hurting the most?" she said.

"Apart from my ego?" He gave her a rueful smile. "Everythin', but I'm not a whinger."

Darren's athletic frame bore down on her as he limped beside Ellie, the strain pulling across her back, with her knees shaking, and a burning sensation coursing down the side of her neck to her shoulder. They took slow, deliberate steps, stopping every few seconds to skirt the piles of rusting scrap metal, Ellie knowing that if she left him now, his look of anguish would haunt her forever. She kept looking back, expecting to see Braddon standing, watching her, the gun rising, the shot firing, Ellie's heart jumping. Darren cleared his throat, and as she looked up at him, he shook his head.

"Just keep walkin'," he said. "If he gets out I'll deal with him."

They reached the steps, and Darren looked back, with a hint of suspicion in his eyes. He didn't give away his thoughts, but Ellie guessed that when Darren locked Braddon in the toilet, over three quarters of an hour ago, Braddon's arm wasn't showing beneath the door.

Darren pushed Ellie in front of him, refusing to take her offered hand, glancing back as he climbed the steps, Ellie watching as he gripped the handrail. She held the door open for him, and then switched on the light, Darren blowing out his cheeks as he passed her. He leaned against the radiator while Ellie locked the door, dumping the huge bunch of keys onto the table. She plucked the first-aid kit and painkillers from the box, then led him to the kitchen sink, exhaling as the colour returned to Darren's cheeks.

He pulled off his sweater with a snarl, Ellie shuddering as the wound opened. She draped his sweater over a chair near the boiler, glancing over the cuts and bruising to his chest. She fidgeted as he watched her, with a dejected expression in his eyes. *He knows just how to make me feel guilty.* Ellie opened the kit, removed the pack of butterfly stitches, and placed them on the table while he swilled the blood from his hands.

Darren nodded towards the pack. "Do you know what to do? I can talk you through it."

"No. It's OK. I know what to do." She smiled and slipped her hands inside the disposable gloves. "I've patched up a few Aussie amateur cricketers this year."

Darren's face lit up. "Yeah?"

Ellie ripped open a cleansing wipe from the kit while he opened his jeans, and she wiped the blood from his skin, Darren's jaw tight and his eyes creasing. He leaned over the sink, holding the edges of the cut together, stemming the bleeding, as Ellie washed it and dabbed it dry. Ellie felt queasy at the sight of blood on her gloves, and she rinsed them beneath the tap.

He looked a little less sick as he hoisted himself up onto the table, perching with his legs open, his keen expression returning as he watched her. Ellie tore open the pack of stitches, and then pulled up a stool, finding it difficult to get close enough to him, blushing when she found herself between his legs.

His eyes sparkled, the corners of his mouth twitching. "Beaut, I can sit on the stool if that's easier for you."

Ellie shook her head. "No. That's worse."

Darren's left eyebrow shot up. "Why?"

"Because then I would have to kneel . . ."

Darren's smile broke into a wolfish grin, and as he winked at her, Ellie felt her cheeks turn a deep shade of pink. She pretended to hunt for the scissors, resisting the desire to meet his bedroom eyes.

Ellie trimmed the adhesive stitches and applied them to the wound, leaving a tiny gap between each stitch, biting her lower lip as she focused while moving his fingers along the wound, with her delicate touch, until she could work without him.

She glimpsed the gentle rise and fall of his bare chest out of the corner of her eye, with his breath stirring her hair, Ellie aware of her sweater pulling tight over her hardening nipples, and of the ridge appearing in his jeans.

She placed the final stitch, and then inspected the wound, pressing, and touching, relieved that the blood no longer seeped out. She placed two horizontal stitches over the vertical strips to hold them in place.

"Try to keep still for a while," she said. "It's a shame that you'll have another scar, but I've tried to make it neat for you."

"No worries." He checked the stitches and nodded his approval. "Good on ya. Thanks, darl'." He dropped another kiss on her forehead.

Ellie slipped down from the stool, pulled off the gloves, and dropped them into the sink, her cheeks, and her skin, tingling. She held a cup under the cold-water tap, sensing his gaze upon her as the water flowed. She turned off the tap and stood, with the cup in her hand, suppressing the urge to turn around and touch him.

She stared through the window, the darkness outside sharpening her reflection in the glass, Ellie holding her breath as she glanced across the courtyard. Braddon's cell door remained closed, and she breathed again. Darren touched her shoulder, and the cup jerked, water splashing over the side.

"Don't keep lookin' out there, beaut."

Ellie turned to face him, passing the cup to him, but he gave it back to her, taking the painkillers without water, swallowing hard. Ellie put down the cup as she prodded the stitches, and then she pulled his hand away, Darren's mouth curving into a smile.

"Wish you'd been around to stop me pickin' at my other scars," he said.

"How did you get the others?" Ellie's gaze dropped to his crotch, the scar hidden again inside his trunks, framed within the open fly of his jeans.

"I crashed at a cross-country rally last year. My co-driver got it wrong, the old bastard." He reached down, rolling up the leg of his jeans, flinching as he bent at the waist.

"What happened?" Ellie tipped her head on one side, noticing the dark hairs on his lower leg, just above the cuff of his boot.

"Dunno. It was a bit of a blur. I reckon I didn't make the turn. I broke my leg, my collarbone, and had a shard of metal cut right into my groin." He couldn't roll the material up as far as the knee, and he unrolled it again, wincing as he stood up straight, checking his stitches before he tucked his thumbs inside the waistband of his jeans. "Couldn't drive for weeks."

"Was your co-driver OK?"

"Nah. He broke both of his legs, smashed his pelvis, and ruptured his spleen. I was lucky, you know." He dragged his jeans down, Ellie biting her lip, the bulge inside his designer trunks taking her eye as he inspected his knee.

Ellie wetted her lips. "How is it?"

"Nothin' broken this time. It's all good."

"It's badly bruised." Ellie trailed her gaze over his muscular thigh, then down to his knee, her heart beating faster when he glanced up at her.

"Nah, it's nothin'."

He drew up his jeans, adjusting his bulge before fastening his fly, Ellie feeling the heat surge through her body, her hands trembling as she tore her gaze from his groin. He reached for his sweater, slipped the arms on first, and then tugged it over his head. He flinched as he put weight on his knee.

Ellie cleared her throat. "Can you still run, if we have to?"

"Four-minute-mile, mate. No worries." Darren glanced down at her, a frown appearing at his brow. "You're lookin' flushed." He felt her forehead, then her pulse, and then the back of her neck, beneath her hair. His touch sent a tremble through her body, and Ellie quivered.

"I'm fine. I'm just tired," she said.

"If it wasn't for Braddon out there, I'd tell you to get some sleep." He took her hand, then led her into the lounge, and switched on the light.

Ellie shied away from the sight of the floorboards smeared with Braddon's blood. "Oh God."

"Sorry, beaut. I didn't clean up."

Ellie sank onto the sofa, her knees weak. She wanted to sleep, a natural sleep, but she knew that he couldn't let her. She unzipped her boots, rubbing her calves, relieved that the awful jeans that Darren snatched were too small for her to wear.

She diverted her gaze from the overturned bookcase, the bread knife jutting out from beneath the sofa, and the trail of blood leading out through the doorway. She leaned back, closing her eyes, and he placed his hand on her knee.

"I need a smoke. Don't go to sleep, beaut."

Ellie nodded. She heard him limp to the kitchen door, heard the cigarette packet crackle as he drew out the last cigarette, and then crush the packet in his hand. She heard the flick of the lighter, and then smelled the smoke as it wafted through the hallway, and into the lounge. She opened her eyes, watching him take a drag, and then he sighed, flicking the ash into the cup on the draining board. He glanced up and caught his breath.

"*Christ.*" Darren backed out of the kitchen, and then turned, with a grave expression in his eyes. He came in, taking her hand, pulling her from the sofa. "We have to leave, now."

Ellie froze. "But what if he gets out?"

Darren reached over her shoulder, and flicked off the light, plunging the room into darkness. "He's already out."

CHAPTER SEVEN

PRECIPICE

Ellie came to an abrupt halt in the kitchen as Darren led her by the hand, her cry lodging within her throat, her skin prickling as she read the word, daubed with blood on the window. Snow spattered onto the disjointed letters, bloodstained snowflakes sliding down the glass outside, backlit by a subtle orange hue as snow clouds gathered overhead. She read the word over and over. *Prey.*

A thud came from beneath her feet, her nerve endings tingling as she looked down at the trapdoor to the cellar, with her hand over her mouth, her eyes wide, and she froze.

"*Darren—*"

"Christ. He's in the bloody cellar." He gripped her hand, pulling her off the trapdoor, his gaze darting around the room, with his eyes wild. He gripped the short edge of the table, leaning into it, the muscles in his cheeks tight, and his jaw clenched. "Beaut, help me."

Ellie ran towards him and pushed alongside him, the table shuddering, scraping along the tiles. It jerked to a sudden stop within an inch of the trapdoor, as the leg struck the edge of a raised tile, with pains shooting from her wrists to her shoulders.

Darren smacked his fist on the table. "*Shit.*"

He hauled Ellie behind him as footsteps crept up the stairs beneath the trapdoor, Ellie holding her breath, with her hands curled tight around Darren's arm. He slammed his foot against the wooden stool, and it fell with a crash across the trap, Darren lurching backwards, colliding with Ellie as the gunshot rang out from the room beneath, Ellie squealing, and her stomach jolting as she hit the wall behind her.

Darren drove the boxes from the table onto the trap, snatching the keys from the floor as they fell. He gripped Ellie's hand, then pulled her to the front door, searching for the key on the fob, his hands shaking, sweat beading on his forehead as he tried one key after another.

Braddon hurled himself against the trap from below, Ellie gasping, shaking, her urethra opening. She squeezed her pelvic floor muscles, but couldn't stop a little spray of liquid escaping into her knickers, her chest muscles tightening as Darren yanked on the handle of the front door. He pulled hard, but the door held fast, the handle springing back in his hand, snapping his fingers back.

"*Shit*." Darren wedged his hand under his armpit, his teeth clamped together, with pain creasing his face.

A worn key stood proud of the others on the fob, and Ellie snatched the keys from his hand. She slipped the key into the lock, but it wouldn't turn, her hands shaking too much. Darren's large hand enveloped hers, twisting it until the key turned in her hand, then he wrenched open the door, bundling Ellie down the steps outside, with the silent snowflakes trickling down around her, and the orange hue dissipating into the darkness.

She ran with him to the car, slipping on the new snow that settled on the thin, frozen layer beneath her feet, with the cold wind biting at her lips. Ellie held onto him, her heart crashing against her ribs as he tugged the car keys from his pocket.

"What if it doesn't start? What if it doesn't start?" she said.

Darren snatched open the rear door and bundled her inside. "Keep your head down."

Ellie lay across the rear seats, her chin quivering, with a tremor in her hands. Darren swiped the wet snow from the windscreen, then hurled himself into the driver's seat. The engine hammered, knocking with every turn of the key, black smoke visible through the rear window, Darren imploring the car to start until he yanked out the key, and kicked open the door. Ellie felt his hands grip her arms, and he pulled her out of the car, the glow from the interior light illuminating his grim expression.

"Can you steer the car if I push it?" he said.

"Why?" Ellie's face drained. "What are you going to do?"

"Trap the bastard in the cellar."

He guided her to the driver's door, and as she ducked into the car and sat down, he inserted the key into the ignition and turned it, Ellie breathing fast as he leaned over her and selected second gear as she pressed down the clutch pedal. He flicked on the headlights, and then he released the handbrake.

Ellie eased off the brake pedal as he pushed the car forwards from the open doorway, with his hand to the steering wheel to help her, Darren's knees buckling, and his feet sliding on the ice with every step. The car rolled forward a little, then he ran to the back, Ellie holding her breath as he skidded in the snow, almost falling, and his arm flailing. He leaned his shoulder against the back of the car, and Ellie tightened her trembling hands around the wheel, turning it to the right, with the angled cellar-doors just visible in the snow, next to the pile of corrugated sheeting. She heard the crack in his voice as he bawled at her.

"As soon as you're against the doors, hit the brakes."

The left-hand door to the cellar moved a little, the barrel of a gun visible within the beams of the dipped headlights, Braddon ducking below the entrance to the cellars as the lights picked him out. Ellie wrenched the key in the ignition, slamming her foot down on the accelerator pedal. The engine shuddered into life, Darren yelling, throwing himself clear as the car lurched forwards, with Ellie's foot to the floor.

Ellie screamed as the bullet cracked the windscreen, smashing through to the rear window as the car ran up and over the cellar doors, colliding with the wall. The engine juddered and stalled. Ellie ripped on the handbrake, hurling herself from the car, falling to her knees in the snow, with her chin bleeding, and her head spinning. Darren raced towards her and jerked her to her feet.

"Christ, beaut—"

Ellie gripped his arms. "Darren, the cottage was once a row of separate houses, with separate cellar doors. If the cellars are now linked, then Braddon will get out."

Darren whipped around, squinting into the dark, glancing from one cellar doorway to the next, before he turned and fled with her, around the side of the cottage, pulling her through the overgrown vegetable garden, the snow ankle deep, brambles tripping her, and Ellie's heart in her mouth.

The open shafts of her boots slapped her legs, and she tried to fasten the zips as she ran, but he wouldn't stop. He dragged her onwards, Ellie hopping, tugging at the zips. She abandoned her attempts as Darren jumped over the stone wall, his gasp loud as he landed, folding himself over with a groan, Ellie making out his shape in the shadows as she scrambled over the wall. Darren took her weight as she fell against him, Ellie scrabbling for a foothold on the loose stones, invisible in the darkness.

He gave her no time to regain her breath as he took her by the wrist, and ran towards the plantation above them, his limp more pronounced, with a sharp pain driving through Ellie's hip. She tried to keep her pain hidden from him, wiping the blood from the cut to her chin with the cuff of her sweater.

The snow abated, with the moon jostling for a place in the crowded sky, illuminating the track above her and she glanced back. She knew that, if he looked up now, Braddon would see her in the moonlight.

Darren turned as a helicopter surged over the brow of the hill, its searchlight sweeping along the contours of the granite ridge, with its downdraught too far away to disturb the vegetation around them. Darren seized her wrist, and whisked her into the refuge of the trees, at the edge of the plantation.

"Is it for me?" She faltered, and hung back, raising her hand to wave. "Are they looking for me?"

"Ellie, no." He snatched her hand down and drew her into the dark, hurting her wrist in his hold. She tried to wriggle free as he took to his heels, but he strengthened his grasp and yanked on her arm. "Bloody stop that."

Ellie thumped his arm. "I could have been rescued. I could be going home."

She floundered as he ran for the deepest shadows, her legs as heavy as set concrete, with her unzipped boots scraping her heels through her thick socks as they slipped up and down.

"Braddon would get to you first, darl'." Darren's breaths came loud as Ellie flailed behind him. "He'd shoot me in the head, and take you away with him. That bullet he fired was for me. He'd got me in his sights."

The helicopter swung westwards, the reverberation of the blades ebbing away as it disappeared into the murk, and Ellie felt the muscles relax in his arm.

Darren yelled out as he tripped in the dark, clutching the trunk of the pine tree beside him. He released her wrist and clasped his hand to his wound, panting. Ellie gave his arm a gentle squeeze, squinting in the darkness.

"Are you OK?" she said.

"Yeah."

"Is it bleeding again?"

"Don't think so."

Ellie felt his fingers enclose her wrist in a firm grasp, and he pulled her hand from his arm. She felt him glance over his shoulder, peering into the trees behind them. Darkness surrounded them, debilitating and claustrophobic, like a tight-fitting mask. Then the screen of his mobile phone lit up in his hand. He flicked on the torch function, and aimed the light over Ellie's shoulder, into the trees, his eyes narrowing, with his expression of pain and anxiety lit up by the blue hue of the screen facing him.

Ellie looked back, her nails digging into his wrist as she held onto him. The trees turned an eerie shade of white as he panned the torch across them, Ellie's hand flying up to her mouth as animals scattered, the torch-light jerking at the sudden movement as it unveiled their hidden lairs. She tried to calm her heart as it hurled itself at her ribcage, and she turned to face him.

"Can you see anything?"

"No. Don't grip me so hard." Darren's brown eyes took on a strange tint in the light from the phone as he stared passed her.

"He'll find us," she whispered. "He's a trapper, and he knows how to stalk. There were animal traps on the counter in the kitchen of the other place. I saw them."

Darren turned the torch on her, Ellie gasping, shrinking back as she shielded her eyes from the vivid white light.

"For God's sake, turn that thing off," she said. She lowered her hand as he lowered the torch, huge circles of light lingered in her eyes, even when she closed her eyelids. Ellie blinked hard.

He turned away, pointing the torchlight in front of him. "Forget the traps," he said.

"I can't."

"I said forget them." His voice carried an edge, but Ellie couldn't see his expression, and she did not dare guess his thoughts.

"Do you think he was scared off by the helicopter?" she said.

"Maybe."

He led her at a slower pace as Ellie rubbed away the circles of light that tracked every movement of her eyes. Ellie hurried along the narrow track between the trees, with the tightness creeping across her shoulders as she imagined unseen hands grabbing her from behind.

The fallen pine needles rustled on either side of her, Ellie flinching as she stumbled after him, animals darting to safety, Ellie closing her fingers tight around his hand as she drew alongside him when the track widened, his masculine frame shielding her from her thoughts. He drew her to the edge of the clearing, ducking down as the moon brightened, pulling her to her knees beside him, Ellie groaning as the pine needles scratched her grazed knees.

"Sorry beaut. I didn't think." He pointed to the dark ridge, visible against the sky. "We're headin' for the top. The moon's out now, so we'll be able to see. D'you think you can do it?"

"But it's so bleak." Her shoulders drooped. "I can't run that far."

"I'm not askin' you to run. I've walked it before."

"In the dark?" Ellie's eyes flashed wide. "Seriously?"

"Yeah." He shrugged. "Did a night hike with some mates. Weather was shit then, too."

"But we're not dressed for this. My toes are numb already." She shook her head. "Please find us another way."

"There's no other way, beaut. You'll be fine. I'll help you over the rough parts. Don't screw me around up there, 'cos there are bogs near the top." Darren shone the torch on her legs as Ellie nursed her sore knees. "You need to fasten your boots else you'll break your neck."

"I tried, but you wouldn't let me stop."

She sat back and reached into her boots, pulling the thick woollen socks over her jeans, then pulled up the zips, wishing now that she had snatched the stolen sweater from the radiator on the way out of the cottage. Sitting in the moonlight, with snow and ice inches from her feet, and Darren's roving eye intent on staring at her cleavage, Ellie felt more than exposed.

"I'm freezing out here," she said.

"Yeah, I know. You should have worn the sweater. I did tell you to."

"I didn't like it." She let her sigh escape. "I hate it out here, and my hands are so cold."

The moonlight highlighted the glint in his eye and the curve of his easy grin. "I've got somewhere warm you could put them."

Ellie's mouth dropped open, and he laughed, rising to his feet, and offering her his hand. She took it, gasping as he pulled her close, her skin flushing, and her nerves tingling as he clasped her hands in his, blowing on them, his warm breath encircling her icy fingers as he eyed her.

"I could do the same for your tits?" he said.

"Darren, for Christ's sake." Ellie drew away, her arms outstretched as he held onto her hands.

"What?"

"You're too fast, just back off."

He dropped her hands, turned away, and then walked out into the moonlight, with his shoulders slumped forward. He glanced back at her, a pained expression in his eyes, and then he strode away, stumbling over the tufts of grass poking up through the snow.

Ellie heard a rustle in the trees behind her, with her skin bristling, and the fingers of fear crawling over her shoulders. She fled after him, with her legs jolting beneath her, Ellie feeling a sudden longing for him in her chest as she neared him.

"Please slow down," she said.

He muttered under his breath, but she couldn't make out the words. A cry broke free from within her as she tripped in her struggle to catch up with him.

He turned. "What's the matter now?"

"I'm hurting, but you just don't care."

"Of course I bloody care."

He limped towards her, nursing his wound. His heavy sigh reached her first and Ellie didn't know what to do with him when he arrived. She wished she hadn't been so dismissive, knowing how much his touch aroused and excited her, those teenage fantasies urging her to enjoy him. Ellie guessed that she shouldn't, not now, not ever, but the overwhelming ache in her breast felt too real, too strong. *Why do I want him so much?*

"Come on. We need to keep movin'," he said.

He marched her along the track that wound upwards through the grassy tufts, the wind whipping across the exposed hillside, chilling her back, a bitter wind that froze her lips, and brought a dull ache to her sensitive, whitened teeth. Ellie clutched at her sweater, clasping the edges of the deep V-neck together in a bunch in her hand, but the wind forced its way inside, and she felt the cold beneath her feet creep upwards, piercing her bones.

"I can't cope with this," she said. "I need to stop."

"No. He could still find us. We need to reach higher ground." He pushed her in front of him, with his hand against her back, edging her onwards. "Keep movin'."

"I can't. I'm hurting everywhere." Ellie sniffed hard, with her hand over her ear to stop the pain as the wind speared her eardrum with each icy gust. Ellie turned, walking backwards, against the wind. "I want all of this to end."

He sighed. "A few more days. That's all."

Ellie's heart leapt. "Then I'm free to go?"

"Yeah, I reckon." He turned his head, avoiding her eyes.

She gave a sudden start. *Would he abandon me out here?* "You wouldn't leave me alone up here, would you?"

"We won't be up here for long unless you keep stoppin'," he said. "Turn around and walk properly."

Ellie turned, yelling out as she stumbled and fell, ricking her ankle, the pain tearing through her foot, and down to her frozen toes. She lay across the tussocks where she fell, stunned and nauseous, pricked by the gorse bush near her elbow, and her face in the heather. His arm came around her as he lifted her to her feet, Ellie groaning as he kneeled, inspecting her ankle.

Darren sighed. "How bad is it? Can you walk?"

"I don't know. It's murder. It feels like a wrench."

She laid her hand on his shoulder, steadying herself, her face hot. *Why am I so stupid? Why do I need saving all the time?* She sighed, her shoulders falling forwards. *I've never felt so frigging helpless.*

Darren looked up. "Did it snap?"

"No. Please leave it alone. You're hurting me."

Darren let go and stood up, rubbing the back of his neck. He glanced up at the dark clouds edging across the moon, and as he dropped his gaze to her, the moonlight vanished. Ellie caught the first raindrop on her arm, and then another, before the thunderous downpour battered her, flattening her hair, with cold streams running down her face and neck. She made out his silhouette as he stood with his head down, and his shoulders hunched against the driving rain.

"Oh Darren, I hate this. We shouldn't be up here. I'm soaked. We should have taken the lane down to the main road."

"No. The lane ran too straight, and we would have been an easy target. He won't follow us up here in this." He felt the sleeve of her sweater. "I left my bloody jacket in Wade's salon. You could have worn it, would have kept you dry."

"Are you sure Braddon won't follow us?"

"Yeah."

He doesn't sound sure. Oh, God. I hope he's right.

He placed his arm around her as they limped through the open moorland, the gorse scratching her legs, with Darren's phone giving out minimal torchlight against the deluge. He wiped the screen on his sweater, and opened the compass app, adjusting their route as they wandered from the winding track.

Ellie's jaw tightened as the pain rampaged through her ankle, Ellie plagued by an ache in her kidneys, with the landscape conspiring to trip her. She hobbled beside him, with her wet hair hanging in limp strands around her face, the rainwater soaking into her jeans, and her sweater clinging to her cold, wet skin.

"Beaut, there's a stone hut on the other side of the hill," he said. "We'll stop there 'til first light."

Ellie gasped. "We're spending the night up here?"

"Nah, yeah."

"What do you mean, nah, yeah, which is it?" she said.

"Yeah."

Oh shit.

The rain poured down in sheets, turning the snow to slush beneath their feet, loose stones rocking underfoot amid the grassy track, throwing her off balance as Ellie struggled, Darren pointing the torchlight at their feet. The horizontal rain spattered her face with stinging blows, soaking her clothes.

"Shit." Darren's leg surged into the stream hidden by the gorse bushes in the dark, the phone falling as he clutched at the bank to save himself.

"Oh my God." Ellie seized his flailing arm and tugged hard, dragging him out, Darren slipping as he climbed back up the shallow bank.

"Jesus. I nearly went arse-over-tit," he said. "Where's the bloody phone?"

Ellie gasped. "You've lost our torch?"

She scoured the ground around her, feeling with her feet, moving away from the stream, flinching as the gorse jabbed her sore knees.

"Shit." His hand closed around her arm. "Stand still. Don't leave the track."

"Why?" Ellie stiffened. "What's wrong?"

"We're on the wrong bloody path," he said. "This place is surrounded by bogs. That bastard stream should be on our right, not the left."

Ellie gaped. "But you had the compass app . . ."

"Yeah, but no map. Couldn't take a readin'. I lost my bearin's."

"For God's sake, Darren." Ellie folded her arms. "Don't you have a GPS app?"

"It's not my phone. Lloyd gave them to us, to track us."

"Doesn't he trust you?" she said.

"Would you?"

Ellie sensed his withering look. "What do we do now?"

"Cross the stream."

"You're joking." Ellie backed off, wringing her hands.

"No. I'm not." The phone crunched beneath his foot. "Bollocks."

Ellie stooped to pick up the phone, her shoulders drooping. The screen had a crack from edge to edge, and even though the torch shone out, and the compass app worked, the finger swipe didn't.

Darren took the phone from her and sighed. "It's screwed."

"But can we still use the torch?"

"Yeah, for now, if the battery doesn't die on me."

He pointed the torchlight across the fast-flowing stream, and led her along the meandering bank, edging passed the gorse bushes, Ellie drawing in her breath at every scratch, Darren playing the tough guy, and pretending that it didn't hurt. He stopped short, and Ellie bumped into him as she slid to a stop on the wet rock overhanging the stream.

"Steady, beaut. D'you think you can jump across from here?"

Ellie knew that she couldn't, not with her ricked ankle, and her skin-tight jeans. He turned to look at her, and then he walked on, sweeping the stream with the light until he stopped again, and held the torch steady. Ellie drew up and stopped beside him. Boulders jutted out of the water, forming natural, rugged stepping-stones, wet and dangerous. *Oh shit.*

"Well?" He shone the torch towards her.

Ellie blinked. She knew, from the sound of his voice, that his small reserve of patience neared its end, and as he lowered his hand, she gave a slow nod, forgetting that he couldn't see her.

"Well?" he said.

"How deep is it?"

"Deeper than usual. I went in up to my knee. The streams come down from the high tors and can turn into torrents without warnin'. If we don't cross now, we could get cut off." He stepped forward. "Give me your hand."

"No. You'll pull me over." Ellie thrust her hands into the tiny pockets of her jeans.

"No, I won't. Give me your hand." He jiggled her elbow, and her hand slipped out of its hiding place, Ellie tensing as he held it tight. "When I say jump, do it."

He didn't give her the chance to back out as he pulled her to the edge, and leapt onto the first boulder, heaving Ellie with him, her haunting cry scaring her more than the pain raging through her swollen ankle as it folded beneath her. She knocked the phone from his hand with her elbow as he caught her, the phone crashing against the edge of the boulder, jamming into a crevice in the rocks below, with the defused light shining across the surface of the bubbling stream, and then the light went out.

"Shit." Darren wavered as they perched on the rock, with his strong arms around her. "It's totally buggered I reckon."

Ellie moaned as she put her weight on her foot, lifting her knee, clutching his arm. She exhaled as the pain subsided, but she tensed when she realised that there were still two boulders left to navigate.

"I'm sorry. I didn't mean to knock the phone out of your hand," she said. "I can't jump again. I thought I'd broken my ankle this time."

"Wasn't your fault." He knelt, and Ellie held onto him as he reached for the phone. He grunted as he straightened, and then slipped the phone into his back pocket. "Beaut, get on my back. I'll carry you over."

"No. You'll break your stitches."

"Nah." He stepped into the stream, cussing, Ellie empathising with him as the cold water rushed passed his legs. "Put your arms around my neck, beaut. Come on."

Ellie felt a rush of exhilaration as she slung her arms around his neck, Darren crouching a little as she lifted herself onto his back, with her legs either side of his waist, and his arms hooked around her thighs. She leaned into him, holding on as he stood up, the rain streaming down, drenching her body.

Darren splashed through the stream, evading the boulders in the murk, aiming for the opposite bank, Ellie edging nearer to the water as his knees buckled. She held on tight as he hitched her up, feeling the strain in his neck as his tendons pulled taught against her arms. He blundered into deeper water, Ellie holding her breath as he swayed, but he regained his balance, and with his muscles taut, he reached the bank and let her down, ducking under her arm as she slid off his back. He clambered up the bank, and she gave him an appreciative hug and a kiss on his cheek as he shivered against her.

"Thanks, Darren. That was so sweet of you."

"No worries. I'll do it again if I'm gonna get that reaction." He turned away. "Wait here, and don't move."

He wondered away, following a sheep track between the gorse bushes, Ellie limping behind him, her heart racing as she tried to keep up with him. *I'm not giving him the chance to leave me behind.*

He glanced round. "I told you to wait there."

"Yes, I know. But I didn't want to."

He sighed. "We'll follow this track. It's headin' in the right direction."

"Don't go so fast. I can't see, and I'll fall." Ellie felt for his hand. "Are we near to the hut?"

"It isn't far, but you won't like it." He squeezed her hand in his. "You can't be fussy right now, beaut."

"Why? How basic is it?" Ellie swallowed, sure that she wouldn't like the answer.

"It's just one room. A fireplace, wooden sleepin' platform, rough blankets, hurricane lamp, shovel . . ."

"What's that for?" Ellie frowned, pushing her wet hair off her forehead, sniffing hard, the droplets of rain-water dripping from the end of her nose.

"I thought you were an outdoors kind of girl."

Ellie blinked. "I am. Pony trekking, horse riding, tennis—"

"Shit shovelling? Nah, didn't think so."

Ellie's heart sank, and her head dropped. *If he thinks I'm digging a hole.* She needed to rest her ankle, needed to remove her wet clothes, and needed a drink. Her tongue stuck to the roof of her parched mouth, and her head ached with cold. She guessed she could drink the slush, but there were sheep droppings everywhere. Her bladder ached, and she bit her lip. Her silence may have concerned him for he half turned.

"You OK?" he said.

She cleared her throat. "I need to pee."

"Jeez—" Darren said, through gritted teeth.

"I can't help it. I've got a full bladder."

"We haven't got time for one of your long pisses."

"I can't help that," she said. "It's the rain. It always makes me want to go. I'll wet myself if I don't."

"Oh, Christ."

"Promise you'll turn your back?"

Darren sighed. "Ellie, it's dark. I wouldn't be able to see my own dick, let alone your pink bits."

"You're disgusting."

"Nah. You'll get used to it."

"You've got an answer for everything." Ellie stopped, looking around for shelter, and Darren turned to her.

"If you're lookin' for cover," he said, "there isn't any. Get you knickers down, and I'll cover you."

Oh. My. God.

Ellie peeled down her jeans, the rain slapping her bare legs, her skin stinging as she pulled down her knickers and squatted with her legs open, and her eyes closed, Darren's deep breathing audible above the rain. She felt him move in close, standing over her, with his hands on her shoulders, and his feet apart as Ellie's endless stream ran away from her into the darkness. The hot liquid splashed her skin, and she felt Darren's hold tighten. She bounced a little as her stream stopped, shaking off the droplets.

She looked up. "I've finished. Do you have a tissue?"

"No."

Oh hell. Ellie bounced again and hauled up her knickers, and then her jeans. Her clothes were soaked anyway. She guessed that it didn't matter too much, and she doubted that Darren would mind.

"Jeeze." He pulled her to her feet. "That piss was longer than your last one. Remind me not to stop if you need a shit."

He started forward, and Ellie trudged behind him, with her head down, and a fire in her ankle, rivulets of rainwater finding their way inside her sweater, and then into her jeans.

She shook his arm. "Could we die out here if we didn't find shelter?"

"Yeah, I reckon." His answer came from over his shoulder.

Ellie's head dropped, and she hung onto him, blinded by the darkness. More than once, she kicked his heels, falling into him, Darren cursing, limping more and more until he stopped, and took her by the arm.

"For Christ's sake, Ellie. Walk beside me. The track's wide enough. You keep trippin' me up."

"I don't mean to. I can't see properly." She edged around him, keeping the weight off her ankle.

"D'you think I can?"

"I said I didn't mean it." Ellie's mouth drooped as he led her up the track, walking too fast for her, maybe too fast for his own injuries, she didn't know. "I need to take my boot off. My ankle's hurting."

"No. We've stopped enough times. Leave your boot on, or else it will swell up."

"It's already swollen," she said. "I wrenched it again when I landed on the rock."

"Sorry mate. The boot stays on."

Ellie bit her stinging lip, with her freezing hands curled, and a stabbing pain in her eye socket as the cold gouged a channel within her skull.

The rain subsided as the wind dropped, and Ellie felt the hope rise within her chest before Darren beat it down again with a sudden blast of pessimism.

"If the mist comes down we're totally bloody screwed."

Ellie felt her hope drop away like a boulder going over a cliff as she took in the reality of his words, and she hoped that shelter would come soon.

The dark hulk of the ridge appeared above them as the rain stopped, and Darren pointed ahead. "The ridge on the hill behind is a tough bugger to reach. We can't see it now, but it's higher, and more exposed, you know."

"We're not going up there are we?"

"Nah. I wouldn't do that to you. The hut's not far now, beaut. As soon as it gets light tomorrow, we'll head for the valley on the other side. Downhill, all the way."

Ellie fought the impulse to throw her arms around him with relief as he clasped his fingers around hers, guiding her along the track onto open heathland, the moon parting the clouds, gifting Ellie a little pale light.

She watched as he glanced behind him, the glances increasing in frequency until he stopped and faced her, his eyes narrow, and his head cocked.

"What's wrong?" she said.

"Can you hear that?"

Ellie shook her head. "I can only hear the wind—"

"Quiet." He lifted his fingers to her lips, with his head lowered.

He stood, his breathing steady, Ellie gazing up at him, inhaling the scent of his fingers, with her heart thudding as she strained to hear.

"I still can't hear anything." Ellie peered behind her, hearing nothing and seeing even less. She moved over, looking round the gorse, down into the valley. She wrinkled her nose. "What did you hear?"

"Dunno. Couldn't make it out. Sounded like dogs barkin'." He looked down at her feet. "Oh shit."

Ellie pulled her foot out of the soft earth, the mud sucking at her boot, her foot plunging back into the muck as she overbalanced. Her chest tightened as the mud enveloped her boots up to the vamp, and she felt herself sinking deeper with each effort to free herself, unable to find firm ground. She felt his hands enclose her wrists, and he hauled her out of the marsh, guiding her through the low-growing heathers, and onto firm ground.

"Keep with me, and don't bloody wander off," he said.

"Do I have a choice?"

"I've still got the handcuffs, so don't start."

Ellie's jaw dropped. "After I steered the car for you, and stitched your wound? I could have left you bleeding on the ground outside. I could have run."

"Why didn't you?"

Ellie jerked to a stop, with the heat creeping into her cheeks, and her throat tightening. "He would have killed you."

Darren faced her, rubbing his temple as he pondered her. "You shouldn't care, Ellie."

"You came back to rescue me when you passed Braddon on the road. You didn't have to. You haven't always been . . ."

"Been what?"

A bastard. "Like this. Charlotte told me that you used to be fun. You didn't do crime, and you had a job, a nice car, and everything."

Darren averted his eyes, making an odd noise in his throat, his hand massaging the back of his neck before he maneuvered her in front of him, and drove her up the hillside.

Ellie hoped that he would speak, and when he didn't, she took a breath. "You used to tease me while you were waiting for Charlotte to get ready for a date. You were so nice."

"Nah, beaut. I've always been a bastard."

"You weren't to me."

"You were just a kid back then. You're slowin' me down. Come on." He pushed her forward, his hand on her shoulder, steering her towards the granite tors that glistened above them.

Ellie ducked out of the wind as they reached the outcrop, flopping down onto the nearest flat rock, then slumping forward, feeling her ankle. Darren lowered himself beside her, with his hand on his wound, and his other hand on her shoulder as she sat up with a sigh. His hand transferred to her thigh, and she caught his sidelong glance, her heart racing. She swallowed, watching his expression intensify in the moonlight as she wet her lips.

"Would you rather be doing something else *with* someone else?" she whispered.

"I know what I'd rather be doin' with you."

Ellie felt the thrill ripple through her body. He encircled her waist with his arm, tucking his cold hand under her sweater as Ellie leaned against him, with her knees against his thigh. She clasped her cold hands between her knees, but the soaked denim jeans held little comfort. Ellie's lips parted as he wetted his, her chest rising and falling faster as she gazed up at him.

Darren's gaze shifted, his body tensing, the muscles in his face tightening as he stared down the hill. "Don't move."

Ellie froze. "Why not?"

"Search party. Down in the valley." He pointed back the way they'd walked. "Wait here. I need a better viewpoint from higher up."

Ellie turned, gasping at the sight of the lit procession. Lights veered off to the west, while others split off to the east. She turned back in time to see Darren disappear over the rocks above her.

Ellie stood alone, the quietness, but for the dripping snowmelt around her, enshrined her like an invisible mist, her arms hugging her quivering body, her hands massaging her upper arms. She prayed that he hadn't abandoned her like this. His keenness for her was evident and to stand there, a solitary figure in a wild landscape, brought his name to her lips.

His shadow appeared first, and as he dropped down to the ledge twenty feet above her, he slipped on the wet rock, his body hitting the granite, his legs careering over the edge, his hands scrabbling for a hold as gravity pulled him further over the edge. Darren hung by his hands, fingers gripping, loosening, clawing at the rock, Darren sliding, his face stricken, and his body rigid. He glanced down at the rocks below him, and as he slid further, he let go, Ellie screaming, losing sight of him as he fell.

Ellie scrambled up, over the rocks, calling his name, her stomach knotting as she heard his groan. She found him on his knees, his fingers bleeding.

"Christ, Ellie—" he said.

"I couldn't get to you." Ellie flung her arms around him, knocking him off balance. "You let go of the ledge. I thought you would die."

"I controlled the fall, 'cos I would have cracked my head open. Steady beaut. I've smacked my knee again. Feels bloody weird—"

The sudden roar of a helicopter drowned out his words as the searchlight swept along the valley floor. He pulled her down, into a deep rocky crevice, crouching above her. He slithered down to her, his face inches from hers, and his legs either side of her, with his strong arms holding her against him. His chest heaved as he breathed, and Ellie gripped him, his breath on her cheek, and his gaze darting from scene to scene, with Ellie's heightened sense of awareness picking up on his fear, fuelling her own.

The searchlight held steady, and Darren turned his head, Ellie staring passed him as they watched the figure of a man, clutching the winch, descending from the helicopter, and as the aircraft swung into position, the word *Rescue* came into view.

Darren turned back. "They're airliftin' someone else out of the valley."

"They're not looking for me?" she said.

"No. No one knows you're up here with me, not even Braddon."

Ellie crouched, with her head down, and her forehead against the side of his neck. She could run out, waving, screaming, but Darren held her in an iron grip, both in his arms and in her heart. *Only a few days, just a few more days, then I'll be free.*

The moonlight withered as clouds raced overhead, chased down by the strengthening wind, and as the hail came down, drowning all sounds from the hillside, the rotor blades hauled the helicopter up and away, plunging the scene into blackness.

CHAPTER EIGHT

RUSH

The stone hut loomed up within the shadow of the hill, the outline of its chimney tall against the dark, winter landscape, the slate roof bowed, and the tiny window, shuttered. A shallow pool guarded the hut against the trail, with moonlight rippling across the surface of the pool, and ice forming at its edge.

Darren pushed Ellie through a gap in the boundary wall before he climbed through, swearing under his breath as he landed beside her, with Ellie's hand outstretched to help him. She guessed that his injuries were worse than he let on, and she slid her hand through the crook of his arm as he led her around the water's edge, towards the hut.

The wind dried her lips, froze her fingers, and blew her cold, wet hair across her face. She couldn't feel her toes, just the pulsing of blood through her injured ankle, tight within her boot. Her wet jeans and soaked sweater felt heavy, and as he let her go, pushing open the door to the hut, Ellie hurried inside the tiny building, sinking onto the wooden sleeping platform with a heavy sigh.

He followed her into the hut, the door slamming in the wind, blotting out the moonlight, the hut pitch-black, except for the narrow strip of light filtering between the shutters.

"Sit still, beaut. I'll find the lamp," he said.

Ellie drew her knees up and rested her head on them, hugging her shins, shivering. She heard him move across the tiny room, heard the creak of a cupboard door, the rattle of metal and glass, and then a whining sound.

A glow appeared by the cupboard, and then it brightened as he turned the winder on the hurricane lamp, the whining louder, faster now. The glow highlighted his strained expression, the wild look in his eyes, and the bruising to his forehead before he turned, and then limped to the fireplace. He peered up the chimney, with the lamp beside his head, and then he ducked back into the room.

"It's all good," he said. "We can get a fire goin'."

Ellie glanced around, wrinkling her nose. "What is this place? It's so tiny. Is this what they call a bothy?"

"Not officially." Darren tugged out a pile of rough, grey blankets from the open cupboard, and threw them onto the sleeping platform. "Farmer was pissed off with hikers lightin' fires on his land, so he opened up this place. It's not always open. We broke in last time."

Ellie's eyes widened. "You broke in?"

"'Course we did." He hung the lamp from the hook embedded in the wooden beam above. "Would have broken in tonight if the old bastard had locked it." He picked up the kindling from the hearth, then the poker.

A wet patch formed around Ellie's bottom on the platform, and she shot up, feeling herself through her jeans. She flopped down again with a sigh, resting on the edge, the moisture from her rain-soaked clothes dripping onto the floor. She placed her hand on the scratchy blankets beside her, guessing that they would feel uncomfortable against her bare skin.

Darren struggled to kneel as he lit the fire with his cigarette lighter, his hands red with cold, like her own. His split knuckles still looked raw as he prodded the fire with the poker, but he appeared to have good use of his hands, despite the cuts and grazes. *He won't let anything beat him. And he carried me across the stream.*

She listened to the wind whistling around the hut, and the creaking of the solitary tree outside, with its branches scraping along the slate and stone with every gust. She felt the draught blowing under the door, and smelled the wood smoke as the fire took hold, Darren edging backwards as the fire crackled and spat.

"Half an hour," he said, "and we'll be roastin'."

"I can't feel it from here. I'm freezing."

Darren dropped the metal poker onto the hearth with a thud and came over. He felt her wet hair, and then her sweater, his face serious. His hand hovered over her jeans, and a thrill surged through Ellie's chest as he felt her thigh.

"Beaut, you need to get out of those wet clothes."

Ellie caught her breath as he crouched in front of her and unzipped her boots. "But you said I should keep my boot on," she said.

"Yeah, I know." He tugged at her boot.

She slapped his hand away. "Don't pull it. You're hurting me."

"It's OK. I'll strap it up." He sat back on his heels as Ellie raised her hand again.

"What with?" She folded her arms.

"Trust me."

Ellie snorted, and Darren's eyebrows raised. He produced the flick knife, released the bloodstained blade, then cut a strip of material from the edge of the nearest blanket, before closing the knife and scooting it along the floor towards the hearth. He removed the boot from Ellie's uninjured foot before tackling the other boot.

Ellie gripped his shoulders as he pulled and twisted, the corners of her eyes creasing as the fire in her ankle burned. She felt herself sliding off the platform, but he placed his strong hand against her stomach and yanked off her boot.

Ellie yelled out, gripping her foot, with her knee to her chin, and her teeth clenched. "Shit—"

"Sorry beaut, I didn't mean to hurt you."

"You can't be gentle at all, can you?" Ellie pushed her wet hair off her forehead. "Just leave it alone," she said as he leaned forward. "It doesn't need you to make it worse."

Darren grinned, then tugged off his sweater, with his scars and stitches visible again, accompanied by the new bruises to his torso. He held out his hand, his eyebrow cocked, and Ellie rubbed her temple before gripping the sopping hem of her sweater, and pulling it over her head, exposing her breasts. She heard him draw breath and she swallowed as she released herself from the dripping garment.

Darren carried the sweaters outside, then wrung them out, with the water spraying onto his boots as the wind battered him. He came in, kicked the door shut, and then hung the sweaters over the open cupboard door. He gestured towards her jeans.

"They won't dry as quick," he said, "but I'll give them a fair go."

Ellie squinted, looking up at him, pinching her lower lip with her fingers as he smiled. She breathed out and pulled off her socks, then stripped off her jeans, holding onto her knickers to stop them riding down.

Darren whistled and knelt, with his hands around her swollen ankle, checking it over, and feeling her icy toes. Ellie's cheeks reddened as his head bobbed between her knees. He glanced at the crotch of her knickers before looking up.

"Your ankle's buggered. It's a bad wrench. I'll strap it up as soon as I'm out of these bloody wet jeans."

He stood up, facing her, then removed his biker boots, opened his belt, and dropped his jeans, Ellie staring at the obvious bulge in his trunks as he stepped out of his jeans, and slung them, with Ellie's, near the fire.

He picked up the strip of material and wrapped it tight around her ankle. She watched his gaze travel along her thighs, and then rest between her legs, his pupils dilating. His bulge twitched in his trunks, and Ellie's body tingled. She imagined the dark hair, the length, and the feel in her hands. She felt her nipples harden, and she knew that he'd noticed.

He rose to his feet, and stood over her, with his eyes intense, and his breathing shallow. Ellie watched as his tongue wet his lips, with his trunks pulling taut over his bulge. He ran his fingers through his wet hair, then turned away, Ellie crossing her legs to stem the tingle between them. *Why do I need him so much? Why him? Why can't I hate him?*

"Darren . . ."

"Yeah?"

"How long until I'm free to go?"

"About forty-eight hours. After the drop."

Ellie lowered her gaze to the floor and then across to the fire, the flames entrancing, warming her body.

Forty-eight hours and them I'm free to leave, to go home. Ellie thought of her life, the typical student with a secret following of politicians and executives, smooth talking smart men, with beautiful suits, and expensive cars. She glanced up at Darren, the rugged Aussie bloke, down to earth, strong, flawed, and sexy. Ellie closed her eyes as she remembered her fantasies, Darren naked, walking in on her in the shower, taking her up against the wall, wet, hot, dripping—

"What you thinkin' beaut?"

Ellie jerked, the heat racing up her neck and bursting out through her cheeks, with her stomach tightening. "Nothing. Nothing, I was just thinking."

"About me?" Darren gave her a sidelong glance and reached out, moving her long hair off her face.

He leaned towards her, and as his gaze dropped to her mouth, he cradled the back of her head with his hand and kissed her. Her heart thudded in her chest as she gasped, the fluttering tickling her stomach, and her nerve endings prickling. He kissed her again, harder this time, with his eyes searching hers as he let her go.

Ellie reached up and touched his mouth, feeling the soft, fleshy skin beneath her fingers. He pulled her to her feet, then slipped his arms around her, Ellie pressing her lips against his mouth as he held her close. She felt his tongue slip between her lips, and she melted in his arms.

Ellie planted hot, little kisses on his lips, with her hands to his cheeks, and his designer stubble sharp against the heels of her hands. Ellie's kisses were fervent, sensual and Darren groaned, pulling her hands from his face, holding them, his eyes engaging as she watched him.

"Beaut, if you kiss me like that, I can't hold back."

Ellie peppered his lips with kisses, her breasts pressing against his naked, muscular chest, with her arms around his neck. She felt his shaft pulsating against her through his trunks, and he pulled her off him.

"I mean it, Ellie," he said. "Is that what you want?"

Ellie nodded, feeling a rush of excitement, her stomach turning over, and an ache for him beneath her breasts as he kissed her neck, her throat, and her collarbone. He cupped his hand beneath her breast and placed his lips around her nipple, sucking, pulling, and licking, her skin tingling in his mouth, with her hand on the back of his head, pushing him onto her breast, stroking his neck, and running her fingers through his hair.

She felt his hot breath on her nipples and his hand slipping down to her knickers, his finger under the tiny band, pulling them open, Darren gazing downwards into them. Ellie gasped as he looked up at her with those hypnotic eyes, intense and alluring. She nodded. He pulled her knickers down, tugging them over her ankles, and then slipped his fingers between her legs, Ellie throbbing beneath his touch as he explored her, his fingers stroking, rubbing, and caressing her.

He lay her down on the platform, climbing up beside her, with Ellie responding to his every touch, moaning as his fingers slipped inside her, feeling, curling, and seeking her G-spot, with his grin swift, and his kisses hard.

Darren took her hand and placed it against his bulge, Ellie feeling his erection beneath the fabric, the twitch against her palm, and her overwhelming urge to straddle him. He pulled open his trunks and Ellie reached inside, her hand enclosing his shaft, Darren's fingers slipping in and out of her, Ellie groaning, her knees bending, and her thighs tingling. Ellie's skin prickled as his hand came over hers, and slid her hand up and down his hard shaft, with his skin soft in her palm, and his thick shaft hot and rigid.

He took his fingers from inside her, staring into her eyes, his lips parting, with his fingers between them, tasting her. She caressed his shaft, and as she slid her own finger between her legs, he pulled her hand away, shaking his head.

He slipped off his trunks and parted her legs, Ellie raising them as he kissed her between them, before trailing his tongue over her inner lips, the tip entering her as he nestled between her thighs. Ellie stroked her breasts, her fingers to her mouth as he licked her, his tongue toying with her, darting in and out of her, his breath hot against her skin, Ellie's body rising in her urgent need for his erection.

He pulled her up and kissed her, Ellie tasting herself on his lips, and then he slid his knees either side of her thighs, and pressed his shaft against her mouth. Ellie let him enter her mouth, her tongue teasing, twirling, sucking, Darren gasping, gripping her hair, with small thrusts in her mouth, as Ellie tasted him, with her hands to his hips, and her body desperate to enjoy him.

He pulled out, his eyes piercing, and his hands shaking as he lay her on her back, and as she opened her legs for him, he climbed onto her, opening her with his fingers, and then slid his shaft inside her, Ellie feeling his erection bulging deep inside as Darren rested on his elbows, with his head bent, kissing her. Ellie quivered with each thrust of his shaft as it glided in and out– wet, dirty, raw.

He slipped her legs over his shoulders, and Ellie felt his erection plunge deeper into her, thrusting, urgent, and desperate, Ellie moaning, with his hands gripping her thighs, his eyes wild, and his chest heaving as he pounded into her. Ellie's body rose and pitched with his, throbbing and sucking on him between her legs. He released her thighs, groaning as she folded them around his waist, clinging to him as he thrust harder, faster, kissing her, with his tongue in her mouth, and the lips between her legs swelling as she consumed his length again and again.

She felt his stubble against her cheek, and his tanned chest against her breasts as he gripped her hard. Elation surged through her body, with her legs tight around him, her head back, her muscles trembling, with her neck, her lips, and her face flushed as heat radiated through her body. She quivered as excitement exploded between her legs, and up through her whole body. Darren groaned as Ellie squealed, his thrusts wild, his body tense against hers as he let her climax before spraying inside her.

He rolled onto his back, gasping, with his hand on her thigh, his chest heaving, and his arm across his face. Ellie's heart hammered, and her body trembled as she curled up beside him, resting her head against his chest. He lowered his arm and placed it around her, Ellie wishing that she could lie there forever but she knew she never could.

He lay with her until her breathing calmed, and then he gave her a gentle nudge, moving her off his chest as he blew out his cheeks, and then sat up, reaching for a blanket, and her knickers. He handed her both, then slid off the platform, with his trunks in his hand. He checked his knee, Ellie drawing her gaze from his flaccid member down to his knee, feeling queasy as he moved his kneecap with his fingers.

"Is it bad?" Ellie put her knickers on and then wrapped the blanket around her shoulders. "Like, really bad?"

"Just squeaky. Fluid behind the kneecap. She'll be right." He pulled on his trunks, and Ellie inspected his stitches, with her gentle touch, as he stood up straight.

His hand closed over her fingers. "Leave them Ellie. They're fine."

He pulled on his boots and slung a blanket across his shoulders, pulling it close as the wind blew under the door. He produced a worn thermal mug and a solitary tea bag from the cupboard, and ventured outside, the wind sending crisp leaves skittering towards the fireplace, with the flames juddering in a wild dance as the wind tore at them.

Ellie suppressed a giggle as he closed the door behind him, and she pulled on her socks and then stole to the cupboard, peering inside. She tugged out a metallic-looking pouch, with her eyebrows raising as she read the label. *Ready to eat casserole*. Ellie pursed her lips. *Is this edible*?

The door banged open, then Darren came in, windswept, and shivering, with the blanket sliding off his shoulder, his boots muddy, a mug of snowmelt in his hand, and a grim expression on his face. He pushed the door closed and moved her away from the fire.

Ellie cleared her throat, fighting off the urge to laugh. "Can I have this?" She waved the food pouch in front of him. "Whose is it?"

"Left behind by a hiker, too heavy to cart about, I reckon. You'll have to eat it cold you know."

He prodded at the snowmelt in the mug, and then set it in the fireplace to boil. He found a plastic fork in the cupboard with a prong missing and tossed it to her.

"Thanks," she said.

Ellie tore open the pouch, and gulped down the casserole, shuddering at the chilled contents, but surprised at the pleasant taste. The broken fork proved awkward to use, but Ellie felt too hungry to care, watching as the snowmelt boiled in the mug, hopeful of a hot cup of tea.

"Did you find sugar?" she said.

He smiled. "No, you fussy bugger." He whipped the mug from the fireplace, dropping the tea bag into the water. "No milk either."

Ellie wrinkled her nose, and then finished the casserole, her gazed averted from him as she dabbed her mouth with the corner of the blanket.

"Sorry, I didn't share that with you. I was so hungry."

"No worries." He fished out the tea bag and passed her the mug.

Ellie found the tea too hot to drink and placed it on the platform beside her for a while, blowing across it to cool it down, eyeing him as he removed his boots, and winked at her. When the tea was cool enough, she took a sip but didn't like it much. She drank as much as she could, then passed it to him to finish off.

Darren picked up the lamp and set it down on the platform, before peering into her eyes. "I should have let you eat and sleep before I shagged you."

He picked up the spare blanket, Ellie screwing up her eyes as he dried her hair with it, in his usual rough manner. He rolled the blanket into a pillow, and then spread his cover over the platform.

Ellie lay down, sighing as she rested her head on the makeshift pillow, her shoulders relaxing, and the warmth of the fire reaching her, cosy and snug, until Darren stripped off her blanket and moved her over. Ellie sat up, her lips pursed, and her arms folded until he shook out the fabric and lay beside her, covering them both with the material, pulling her back down, grinning at her, Ellie flushing.

Darren set the alarm on his diver's watch and reached for the lamp. The light went out as he flicked the switch, the room lit by the shifting flames that cast huge shadows around the hut. He lay with his back to her, facing the fire.

Ellie propped herself up on one elbow, eyeing him as he watched the flames, their reflections shimmering in his eyes. He glanced over his shoulder, his eyes softening and he turned onto his back, pulling her down to him, with his arms around her and her face against his neck.

She closed her eyes, comforted by his strong arms and muscular body. She listened to the spitting flames, the roaring wind in the chimney, and Darren's gentle breathing. Her life was on hold, and right now, she didn't care. She guessed that he didn't either.

CHAPTER NINE

SNARE

Ellie brushed the early morning frost from the metal rungs of the field-gate, and then leaned back against it, scratching her name in the ice beneath her feet with the toe of her boot, her hands tucked underneath her sweater, and her breath visible in the cold air. She glanced at Darren standing a few feet away, with his hands in the pockets of his filthy jeans, and his brow furrowed as he glanced up and down the empty country road. His hand rose to the back of his neck in slow motion, his eyes troubled as he turned towards her.

"We're too bloody close." His breath came in clouds as it met the cold air.

Ellie stopped scratching. "Too close to what?"

"Wade's cottage. We should be way over there." He pointed over Ellie's shoulder, into the distance. "Miles further to the south."

Ellie gaped, her eyes wide. "We've followed the wrong trail off the moors? We did all of that walking for nothing?"

"Yeah." He dropped his gaze to the road, his shoulders sagging.

"But you've been here before, you've hiked all over. You said you knew—"

"Yeah, OK. Leave it," he said.

"Leave it? You're kidding. You said we'd be safe. What the hell do we do now?"

He looked up. "Steal a car, I reckon—"

He whipped round at the sound of a vehicle speeding towards them. He turned to run, shouting a warning, but Ellie froze, her hands flying to her face, with her chest tight, and her heartbeat thrashing in her ears. The familiar pickup truck skidded around the bend towards them, scraping along the chevron signs with a metal-on-metal shriek, with Darren caught in its headlights.

Ellie cried out as Darren slipped on the ice and crashed to his knees, the truck hurtling towards him, Darren cowering, with his arms across his face. The truck thundered sideways, severing Ellie's view before it crunched to a stop six inches from her trembling body. She sank to her knees as fear robbed the strength from her legs.

Ellie screamed as Braddon hurled himself across the transmission and down from the cab, his large, brutish hand around her throat, Ellie writhing, and squirming, beating him with her hands. He slammed her against the truck, her back arching as the door handle jabbed into her vertebrae, the gash in his forehead glued in a macabre repair, with his fingers squeezing her larynx as he pressed his blood-encrusted cheek against hers, and whispered in her ear.

"Stop that fucking noise, or I'll tear you apart."

He heaved her into the truck, Ellie struggling, and sobbing, kicking out at him until he punched her chest, and locked her inside the truck. Ellie jerked the door lever, her fingers clawing at the window as she tried to force it down, and her ribs sore. Her eyes filled with tears, and her body trembled as Braddon disappeared behind the truck. *If I can't get out now, I'll die.*

She heard Darren's sudden cry of pain, her heart jolting, her search for his reflection in the wing mirror finding him lying on the ground, a few feet from the rear wheels, as Braddon rained blows to his stomach, with a boot to his ribs, and a kick to his groin.

Braddon disappeared from Ellie's view, then wrenched open the driver's door, and threw himself into the seat beside her, the door slamming, and his eyes piercing. He thrust the truck into reverse, yanking Ellie back in her seat, lunging across her to see through her window, and then the wing mirror.

"Where's that fucking bastard?" He swung back to the wheel, ducking to see through his wing mirror before releasing the clutch. "Got him, the fucking shit."

The truck surged backwards, Ellie squealing, clutching at her chest, with her hands clenching. She saw Darren's reflection lurch away as Braddon's gaze jerked from mirror-to-mirror, with his eyes wild, and his nostrils flared, bleeding.

His voice rose in an uncontrolled scream. "Where the fuck is he?"

Ellie jerked his hand from the wheel, but he punched her jaw, her head reeling, with her vision blurred for a second. Her knee juddered against the gear lever, the tremor spreading throughout her body, her jagged nails digging into her clammy palms, with her jaw clenched, and her head spinning.

Braddon spun the truck in an arc, searching the mirrors, Ellie clinging to the door pull, praying that Darren had escaped, but he came into view as the truck slid on the ice, his body slumped against the gate, with his eyes closed, and his face creased. Braddon curled his fingers around the gear lever, his mouth salivating, his prey within his sights.

"Darren, run." Ellie's voice cracked, and she knew he hadn't heard her. She watched, helpless, as he opened his eyes and retched.

Braddon floored the truck, Darren yelling out, dragging himself up from the floor, then mounting the gate in a frantic scramble. He threw himself over, with his arm hooked through the rungs as he fell to the ground on the other side, with the truck scraping along the gate, Darren snatching his arm away. The truck skidded to a stop against the hedge, with Darren hidden from sight.

"*Fucker*," Braddon yelled.

Braddon rammed the truck into first gear, whipping off the clutch, the wheels spinning, smoke billowing from the tyres, with the vile smell of heated rubber entering the cab. Ellie sobbed from her heart, gripping the double seat beneath her, with her eyes wide, and the taste of burning rubber merging with the bile in her mouth.

The truck sped along the icy road, sliding, skidding, with its engine whining. Braddon's breaths came fast with bubbles of blood from his nostrils bursting with every breath. He gave a long, vile snort before spitting bloodied mucus from his mouth, Ellie retching as it spattered onto the steering wheel, and then slithered down, hanging in a slimy, elongated globule above his thigh.

"Oh Christ. Let me go. Let me out." Ellie shook the door lever, slamming her hand against the door panel. "Let me out. You evil bastard."

The truck swerved as Braddon jerked his head, Ellie surging forwards. He gripped her shoulder and slammed her back in her seat, her head striking the headrest, and her teeth clattering together. He jerked her forward by the arm, his dead stare flitting between Ellie and the windscreen as he drove, his mouth twisting into a snarl.

"You're going nowhere, you bitch. I've got plans for you." His hand slid around to the back of her neck, and he curled his fingers, squeezing, holding her in a paralysing grip. "My bitch escaped before she gave birth, but you won't." His eyes pierced her heart. "You'll have my babies." He thrust her head down, Ellie squealing. He tightened his fingers. "I hold grudges, Ell. You glassed me, and you'll pay for it."

Ellie's heart froze over. Her stomach hardened beneath her hand, with vomit hurling into her mouth, and she swallowed hard, breathing deep, with her muscles rigid. She gasped as he forced her head into his lap, the gear lever jamming against her stomach, and the engine racing in the wrong gear. He caressed the nape of her neck, pressing her face into his groin, with the smell of Ellie's stale urine lingering on his trousers, and the gob of mucus hanging from the wheel, just above her cheek.

"I loaded spyware onto Darren's phone." His finger slithered down her spine. "I know where he goes, and what he does." He stopped talking to breathe, then snorted, gulping down the mucus. "I heard him screw you. Suck me, Ell."

"Fuck off."

Braddon's fist came down on the back of her head, Ellie's face hitting the hard bulge in his trousers, with an ache surging over her head. Ellie jerked her head from his lap, striking her cheekbone on the steering wheel, with the gob of mucus sticking to her cheek, her stomach heaving as she swiped the goo from her face, frantic to rid herself of his bloodied phlegm. She dragged her fingers along the seat cover, her body shuddering.

She felt the punch to the side of her head, her body careering sideways, with her ear thick, and sounds dulled for a moment. She sat with her head in her hands, her eyes turned from him, and her breathing sharp, then she heard him reach into the door pocket beside him.

"Darren left this for me," he said. "It's for you."

She felt the scratches on her arm, and as she lifted her head, she reeled at the sight of the hypodermic needle. *Shit. He found the syringe.*

The truck shuddered to a stop as he parked on the grass verge, and Ellie's blood drained from her face as he bent towards her, and felt for the lever beneath her seat. The double seat slid back, his wild, staring eyes inches from hers.

He gulped down the blood from his nose. "On the floor, now."

He forced her into the foot well, with her legs crushed beneath her, and her arm outstretched across the transmission. He tore the ripped sleeve from her sweater, and glared down at her from above the steering wheel as her body shook, her throat tightening, strangling, and her heart pounding, with pearls of sweat forming across her forehead, and her goosebumps rising.

He jabbed the needle into her arm, bursting the skin, Ellie cringing at the sharp, stinging pain, her blood oozing out, and her arm feeling heavy as he emptied the syringe into it. He drew out the needle, then threw it like a dart at her legs, with the tip of the needle stabbing her thigh through her jeans. She gripped the syringe, and snatched it from her thigh, holding it like a dagger above his leg, but he wrestled it from her and struck her mouth. Ellie cried out as her head hit the door of the glove compartment.

She struggled to pull herself up onto the seat, but the drug surged through her veins and numbed her. She slumped forwards, with her head resting on the seat, and her gaze lowered to the gear lever, her bitter tears flowing, distorting her view. She raised her heavy eyelids, looking up into his eyes, shrinking back as the leer spread over his face. She felt consciousness drain from her mind as his face cracked into an expression of joy.

The rasping sounds kept coming, faraway sounds, coming closer as she breathed. She opened her eyes, her vision blurred, with an ache in her head, Ellie lying back in her seat, way back, as the truck rumbled along the lane. She closed her eyes, disoriented, and dizzy, listening to her rasping breaths, and she gulped, lubricating her dry throat and furred tongue.

She felt chilled, feeling her cold, bare legs beneath her hands, then she smelled him, smelled his stench all over her, with her jeans and knickers down her thighs. She moved, then felt the sharp metal scrape against her legs.

Her eyes snapped open, with her breath catching in her throat, and her body rigid. Animal traps lay primed, either side of her thighs, and between her legs. Vicious metal jaws, with their springs taut. The sob forced its way out of her throat, and her urethra leaked. The wail rose from deep within her chest, uncontrollable, and haunting.

Braddon raised his phone, the truck veering as he took photographs of her, Braddon snorting, swallowing, with a gleam in his eyes. He lowered the phone to his lap, pressing the screen with his fingers, his smile widening as the phone pinged its notification onto the screen, and then he sat back, his grin disappearing in an instant.

"You won't leave me," he said. "No matter how much you want to."

He gripped her thigh, driving one-handed, with the truck lurching, bumping over potholes, the traps sliding against her, a snare hanging from the padded ceiling above, swinging in front of her face.

"Oh God." Ellie sat rigid, her chin quivering. "Please don't do this to me."

"The soldering iron," he said, "drags the skin, like this." He dug his fingernail into her thigh and scraped it down to her knee, Ellie flinching, her cries catching in her throat, with the welt hot, and sore.

"Don't hurt me," she whispered.

"The next time I drug you, I'll use the iron . . ."

Ellie died on the inside. She eyed the vile traps, and the soldering iron, rocking in the cup holder between the seats, with its twelve-volt adapter swinging from the end of its cable. A gun lay on the shelf below the dashboard, and she knew that no one could save her. Darren couldn't, and she knew that the police didn't even know of her kidnap. The trap between her legs glistened with the dribble of urine, Ellie staring, dissecting its workings in her mind, with her eyes tracing its spring mechanism, her eyes narrow.

She looked up through the windscreen at the tree tops, the clouds, and the early morning light. From her distorted viewpoint, she made out the rocky tor of the hillside that she had descended earlier with Darren. She hadn't been out cold for long, and she knew that Braddon hadn't driven far. *If Darren can track Braddon's phone, he'll find me.* She guessed that Braddon would think of that, and even as his phone rang, Braddon's window slid down beside him.

"Pretty boy Darren's got your pictures," he said. "He's ringing. He'll try to find you, but no one ever will."

He held the phone outside, and then opened his hand. The phone clattered against the side of the truck, and fell away, with Ellie's gut aching as he severed her only hope of being traced. The window slid upwards, closing with a thud, and Ellie knew that only she could save herself now.

Ellie's skin crawled beneath his hand as he stroked her thigh. She swallowed, and then breathed in deep, forcing a fake smile as she took his hand in hers. The truck swayed, and Ellie's strained smile widened. Braddon's face lit up as Ellie stared into his eyes, pulling his hand towards her groin, Braddon struggling to drive as she pushed his fingers against her lips. He salivated, the ridge reappearing in his trousers, his eager, desperate expression turning to horror as Ellie rammed his hand into the trap between her legs.

His bones crunched and snapped, his blood spurting over her limbs, his screams piercing, with the tendons in his neck pulling tight, and his teeth bared. The truck surged to the side, colliding with the hedge, before bouncing back into the road, the traps sliding forward, with the snare swinging over her face. She ducked beneath it, then snatched the wheel round, slamming the truck into the low stone wall beside it, the back whipping round on the ice, and the engine screaming. Ellie's body crashed against the door, the trap jamming between the door and the seat, its teeth sinking into the fabric, a quarter of an inch from her leg.

She tried to pull on the handbrake, but the other trap lay across it, with its jaws open, hungry for flesh, and spattered with blood. She thought it was her own until she saw the blood running down Braddon's arm, dripping onto the trap. Her hand shot to her mouth, her eyes bulging as he sat, slumped over the wheel, the glued gash oozing blood, and his eyes closed.

Ellie pulled up her jeans, his blood smearing along her thighs as the tight denim slid over her legs, Ellie shuddering. She pushed on the passenger door, but it hit the wall, and wouldn't open more than a few inches. The sprung trap grazed her elbow, and Ellie knew that to escape, she would have to climb over him.

Her gaze swept along the dashboard, searching for the door release. She watched Braddon's blood trickle over it, dripping onto the gun barrel poking out from the shelf beneath. Ellie bit her lip, stealing a look at his ashen face before she reached for the gun, feeling the weight, and the cold metal against her palm. She raised it to head height, turning it on Braddon, with her fingers on the trigger, and her other hand supporting her elbow. She pulled off the safety catch, and held her breath, with her jaw tight. The gun wavered as the tremor in her hand escalated along her arm.

Her fingers curled, the trigger tightened, and her lower lip trembled as she willed herself to pull the trigger, but paralysis gripped her fingers, with her heart racing, and her throat closing. Sweat ran down her forehead, her skin burning up, and she lowered the gun, a heavy sigh rushing out of her chest, and a choking sob breaking from her tightened larynx. *I can't do it. I can't kill him.* She sat with hands over her face and the gun across her lap. She struggled to swallow, struggled to control the surge of panic gripping her chest as she raised her head, and saw him twitch. *Oh shit.*

Ellie gripped the gun and edged forwards, lifting her foot over the transmission, and onto his seat, dry heaving as she pushed him further over the wheel, and inched her knee behind him. She looked back, her eyes widening as her other knee scraped along the edge of the primed trap between the seats. She raised her leg, with her hand on his back to steady herself, gasping as she felt him take a breath beneath her hand.

She wriggled behind him, with her hand out, reaching for the door pull. She pulled hard, but the door wouldn't budge. She yanked it, her mind reeling as it held fast, with silent tears slipping down her cheeks. She slid back, leaning over him, with her fingers slipping in the blood as she pressed the door switch on the dashboard. She heard the reassuring thud of the door catch releasing, her fingertips covered in his sticky blood. She gurgled, wiping her fingers on his clothes, then eased passed him, reaching over, pulling the door lever.

The door clicked open, and she pushed hard, with the cold draught blowing around her, and fresh air racing into her lungs, as she felt for the ledge outside with her foot. She dragged her other leg behind his back, but he slumped backwards, trapping her foot behind him.

Oh Christ, no. No. Ellie pulled and tugged, gripping the doorframe, the gun clanging against the metal frame, with her breath catching, and her face creasing. She twisted her injured foot round, and eased it from under him, slipping off the step, and falling into the road, with the gun beneath her. She lay, winded, with the world rotating, and a raging pain in her ankle.

She pushed herself up, eased the door shut, and then picked up the gun, clicking on the safety catch before wiping her eyes, and looking around, dazed. *What do I do? What do I do?* A sound from the truck startled her, but Braddon lay slumped in the driver's seat, bleeding, and out cold.

Ellie turned on her heel, and ran back along the road, with her eyes down, searching for Braddon's phone. She slipped on the ice, jolting her body, with her arms out, stopping the fall. She heard the ringtone, and ran towards the sound, finding the phone face down in a tractor rut filled with ice and frozen mud. She scooped up the phone, with an unknown number displayed on its scratched screen, then, holding the grubby phone as close as she dared to her ear, she accepted the call.

"Help me," she whispered. "Please get help for me."

"Ellie?"

"Darren?" The phone slipped from her shaking fingers, falling face down onto the ground with a slap, and then slid into the tractor rut. She cried out, snatching the phone from the ground. "Darren?"

"Beaut? Where are you? Where is he? Are you OK?"

"Oh God, I don't know where I am. I don't know. I don't know."

"Where is he? Are you alone? It's OK. I can trace you."

"I crashed his truck, and he's out cold. Please, come and get me. Darren, I'm scared. He drugged me—"

"Listen. I'll get to you. Keep the phone switched on."

"But you don't have a car—"

"Don't talk now else you'll give me away. I've got the chance of a steal. I'll get to you. OK?"

Ellie forced her way through a gap in the hedge, hurrying across the edge of the field, looking for cover. She listened to Darren's breathing as he walked, over crunching ice, to a vehicle with its engine running. She heard him open the door, then slip inside, and then drive away. Her heart sank, empathising with the car's legitimate owner who, perhaps, left the car defrosting, while waiting indoors.

She knew that she had to stay close to the road for Darren to find her. *I know he'll come.* She knelt beside an empty trough, her legs shaking, and her body aching all over. Her bare arm hurt in the cold breeze, with a bruise forming around the puncture wound. She smelled Braddon's stench on her clothes, on her skin, and she shuddered.

The gun lay on the ground by her knees, with the barrel pointing away, its shape leaving an imprint in the frost. She watched the sun disappearing beneath heavy snow clouds piling in from the east, and then she looked down at the gun. *I could be sitting here now with blood on my hands. I could have committed a cold-blooded murder.* She closed her eyes, with her shoulders slumped, and her head down.

Over thirty minutes had passed before Ellie heard the sound of a vehicle above the strengthening wind, and she staggered to her feet, jumping as the phone rang, Ellie recognising Darren's number before it cut off. She pushed herself through the hedge into the road, gasping as the two-door hatchback swerved to avoid her as Darren pulled up.

Ellie dragged open the passenger door, but it swung wide and hit her, the phone slipping out of her hand as she stopped the gun from falling. She dropped to her knees, feeling for the phone under the car.

"Leave it," Darren said. "Get in."

He caressed his ribs as he held out his other hand for the gun, his face ashen, and his cheek bruised. She passed him the gun as she sat beside him, and then pulled the door shut, her eyes brimming with tears. She turned to him as the car pulled away, Darren wincing at every gear change.

He eyed her, his face serious. "Beaut, I drove passed his truck on my way here. You said he was out cold?"

"Yes. He's slumped back in his seat."

"He isn't now," Darren said. "When I drove passed, the door was open, and there was no one in the truck."

CHAPTER TEN

DRIVE

The horizon ebbed into the mist as the snowflakes caught on the wind, whipping upwards then falling, spattering onto the glass, the windscreen wipers bulldozing through them. The moorland road, a snow-covered ribbon of asphalt, stretching away between low stone walls, guided the car along its serpentine route into the wilderness.

Darren cleared the mist from the windscreen, with a vigorous, circular hand movement, while Ellie sat with her hands in her lap, picking the skin around her nails, her breathing steady as she watched the snowflakes ganging up against the wipers, falling faster, settling on the untreated road.

The fleece jacket stretched tight across her chest, with the zip fastened up to her chin, Ellie cocooned in softness. She stroked the cosy material, and eyed Darren as he drove, his sweater torn and dirty, with his jaw tight, and his expression serious.

"I love this jacket," Ellie said. "But it wasn't ours to take."

"I didn't rob it off the woman's back. It was already in the car." He shifted in his seat. "She'll miss the car more than the bloody jacket."

Ellie empathised with his pain. She hugged herself, flinching as she caught her injection site. "Do you think she's called the police?"

"Yeah." He changed gear with his leg outstretched, the pain creasing his face.

Ellie faced him. "Did she see you?"

"Doubt it." He switched on the headlights, with hot air blasting from the heater as he flicked another switch. "I've got to keep drivin' else we're screwed."

Ellie's eyes widened as she leaned forward. "No one's been up here for hours, and the road isn't gritted. Will it get worse? Can you drive in this?"

"'Course I can." He slowed the car using the gears as they approached the brow of a steep hill, with the wipers juddering across the windscreen. He jerked his head. "Sit back, beaut. The car might slide."

Ellie pressed herself back in her seat as Darren changed down into first gear, and then let the weight of the car edge the vehicle downhill, the car picking up speed, avoiding the wall on the bend in the road, with Darren's rally driving skills evident.

Ellie gazed at him. "Is that why Alistair Lloyd chose you to be his getaway driver? Because you're a rally driver?"

A drop of sweat ran down to his cheekbone from his temple before he wiped it away with the back of his hand. "Beaut, lift my sweater. Check my stitches for me."

"Why, what's wrong?" She raised his sweater, gasping at the sight of the inflamed scar beneath the stitches, and the severe bruising to his ribcage. "Oh my God. Braddon did this to you?"

"Beaut, don't fuss." He jogged her arm as he turned the steering wheel. "Just check the stitches."

"They're OK, but I think your wound's infected." Ellie lifted his sweater above his nipple, eyeing the deep purple bruising that wrapped around his chest and back. "Does it hurt when you breathe in?"

"Hurts all the bloody time." He sucked in his breath as Ellie touched his ribs. "Don't touch it while I'm drivin', for Christ's sake."

Ellie lowered his sweater, then tugged her lip as she frowned. "You need a cold compress. We need to collect some ice."

"I've tried that. It didn't work on my balls either."

"Braddon's a bastard." Ellie slumped back in her seat. "Why did you take this . . . job?"

"Money, beaut." His breath escaped in a rush. "I've got huge gamblin' debts." His diver's watch loosened as he turned the wheel, and he slid his watch from his wrist, dropping it into Ellie's lap. "Do somethin' with that."

Ellie studied the watch. Its silver face, with sub dials and digital readouts, stared back from within its chunky casing and rubber strap. She stroked the cold glass, and felt the weight of the watch in her hand, with the warmth of his wrist lingering on the back plate.

Darren glanced over. "Don't set the alarms, and don't touch the bezel."

"Bezel?" Ellie frowned, turning the watch over then back again. "What's that?"

"The bit that rotates. Tells me how long I've got left underwater."

"You actually dive then?" Ellie turned, her eyebrows raised. "You know, proper diving gear, dry suit, and everything?"

"D'you think that I'd take a small mortgage out on that thing if I didn't?" He wiped the mist from his window. "I turned down a dive to do this fuc . . . friggin' job." He ran the back of his hand over his sweating forehead, wincing as he raised his arm.

Ellie tucked the watch into the pocket of the jacket and pulled the zip closed over it, a warm, fuzzy feeling in her stomach now that she had an item of his in her possession.

She imagined him playing poker in a smoky den, with a cigarette hanging from his lip, charming his way through the game as he cheated, spiralling further into debt, laughing off his losing streak. Her inward cosiness faded, for his need for money had almost cost Ellie her life, but then, if Darren hadn't been involved and intervened, and Braddon, her only captor, she would have bled to death in the cellar. Her involuntary shiver spread out from between her shoulder blades, and she wrung her hands in her lap.

"Has Doug paid the ransom?" she said.

He wiped the sweat from his face with the sleeve of his sweater. "No."

"What?" Ellie's hand rose to her throat. "Why not?"

"Knowin' Doug, he's blackmailin' some poor bugger to raise it." Darren shrugged. "He'll pay."

Oh Doug, pay out, please.

Ellie watched Darren change down through the gears. The car slowed to a crawl, and he steered the car into the middle of the road, avoiding the snow building up at the roadside. Large snowflakes poured from the grey sky, adhering to the windows, Ellie tensing as the snow closed in.

"What will you do if Doug goes to the police?" she said.

"He won't, I told you," he said. "He has too much to hide. Taking on Lloyd is suicide. You should know that, studying journalism or whatever. It would do you both good to keep your mouths shut."

"But Lloyd will get away with this." The adrenaline tingled through her body, stinging the palms of her hands. "He can't. He just can't."

Darren shrugged. "He will. That's how it works. You can't beat him, beaut. He's too powerful. I took a chance comin' back for you."

"Will Braddon back off once the ransom's paid?"

He eyed her. "I doubt it. You broke his trigger fingers. He'll make you suffer. A ransom won't stop him now, Ellie. If he gets you back, he'll never let you go."

The shiver rippled all the way up to the nape of her neck as Ellie stared out at the white, swirling snow, driven by the bitter wind, with her mind a blank emptiness, an ice-cold white out. Like the scene before her.

A white van hurtled out of the blizzard, aiming straight for the car, its headlights blinding, and its horn blaring. Ellie cried out as Darren whipped the steering wheel around, snow spraying over the bonnet as the car surged into the drifts, scraping along the stone wall, with the impact forcing the car back into the path of the oncoming vehicle. The van swerved, clipping the rear wing with a heavy bang, spinning the car, Darren wrestling to control it as the wheels skidded beneath them.

Ellie held her arms tight across her stomach, her seatbelt locking her into her seat, with her eyes shut tight until Darren stopped the slide, with the car coming to rest facing back up the road. The van skidded away, dragging its front bumper along the ground, with its red taillights fading as the van disappeared into the blizzard.

"The bastard." Darren released his seatbelt, kicked open his door, then stepped outside. The snow, driven in by the wind, melted on his seat in an instant as the heater blew hot air through the cabin.

Ellie let her seatbelt rattle back into its slot beside her, and then she opened her door. She stepped into the snow that swirled around her, wetting her hair, as she pushed the door closed, with a heaviness in her heart when she saw the damaged paintwork, and she felt for the owner. She trudged through the snow to the rear of the car, her knees shaking, with Darren already on his haunches, pulling the wing about as he freed the rear wheel from the crumpled metal, with snow settling on his sweater.

He looked up. "Beaut, get back in the car. It's too cold out here."

Ellie's hair whipped her face in the wind, stinging her skin. She crouched with him, the rear of the car sheltering her from the weather.

"How bad is it?"

Darren manhandled the bumper. "Could have been worse. It's drivable."

He pushed his hand up into the wheel arch, his cheek against the car, with his gaze on Ellie. He felt around the top of the wheel, and his eyebrows raised. He drew out a chunk of compacted snow, and flung it on the ground, before pushing himself up from the side of the car.

He hoisted her up, brushing the snow from her hair, before placing his cold hand against her cheek. "OK beaut?"

Ellie nodded, then waited while he inspected the wheels. He opened the passenger door, and Ellie sank into her seat, with snow falling from her boot treads onto the mat as she slammed her door.

Darren clambered around the front of the car, and then groaned as he sat down beside her. He pulled the door closed, muttering under his breath as it caught on the seatbelt buckle, bouncing open again. He snatched up the seatbelt, reaching for the door, and then slammed it, squeezing his eyes shut with pain, slumping forwards with his hand over his abdomen.

Ellie clutched his arm. "What's wrong?"

"I'm OK. It's just a twinge." He sat up with a groan, with his hand on the gear lever, and his face red. He put the car into gear, and then cleared his throat. "Put your belt on."

Ellie pulled her seatbelt from its housing and clicked it into place as Darren eased the car onward, with the front wheels grinding, and the car edging forwards as Darren coaxed it away from the drifts. He flicked on the rear windscreen wiper, and turned around in his seat, with his arm on the back of it, hindered by the headrest, as he peered through the rear window.

"Hold tight, beaut. I've got to turn the car," he said.

He reversed the car, slow at first, then he accelerated, swinging the front around, the car bumping over the rutted snow, facing forward, Ellie giddy, with her hand to the dashboard in front of her, and her heart racing. Darren turned back to the wheel, with his arm across his chest, and his teeth clenched as he steered.

"Watch out." Ellie reached for the grab-handle above her, holding on as the car veered towards the low wall.

Darren swung the wheel. "Shit. The bloody fuel light's come on."

Ellie stiffened. "You're not driving over the moors with the fuel light on?"

"No." He corrected the steering, feeling inside the pocket of his jeans.

Ellie frowned as he patted his other pocket. "Then where are we going?"

"Buckfastleigh." He let out a deep sigh, and jerked his head towards the glove compartment. "The woman was a smoker. Look in there, and see if she's left me a smoke."

"Why can't we drive down the main road?" Ellie opened the glove compartment, peering inside.

"Cops are lookin' out for this little motor," Darren said. "We're sneakin' in through the back door. Don't fret. It won't be this bad down there."

Ellie drew out a packet of cigarettes and held it out to him, closing the compartment with a loud snap. "Are these OK for you?"

Darren glanced down, nodded, and tapped her hand away. "Open them for me, beaut. I'm drivin'."

"For God's sake."

Ellie unwrapped the cellophane, flipped open the lid, and drew out a cigarette, pushing it into his hand as he reached over. He stroked her thigh, with a faint smile on his lips, before he snatched his hand back to the steering wheel as the wheels spun.

He drove a few hundred yards before he lit the cigarette, and then took his first drag, with his eyes half closed, and a look of relief spreading over his face. He gave her a sidelong glance, his eyes hypnotic as he breathed out, and Ellie held her breath as the smoke wafted towards her. Darren jerked the window down beside him, and then flicked the ash through the tiny gap.

The road levelled out, and Darren pulled the phone from his back pocket, glimpsing the screen before he screwed up his mouth, with the tip of the cigarette rising towards his nose, before he dropped the phone onto the dashboard, and then took the cigarette from his lips. Ellie reached for the phone, but he seized her hand.

"No, Ellie." He pushed her hand back onto her lap.

"But Braddon said that he bugged your phone. There's spyware on it. He knows everything about you. He knows who you call, and who you speak to. And he heard us . . ." she said, "in the hut."

Darren's eyes widened. "He's trackin' me? He heard us shaggin'?"

Ellie clutched his arm. "Darren, turn the phone off. If he's found his phone, then he knows where we're going."

"I can't. I'm waitin' for the call." He lifted the phone from the dashboard and dropped it into the door pocket beside him. "I can't turn back now, not in this. There's only enough fuel to get into town."

"But I crashed his truck. He can't follow us now."

"Darl', his truck's still drivable 'cos you didn't crash it head on. It won't stop him."

"I had to grab the wheel when I could, and I didn't aim it full on." Ellie's voice caught in her throat. "I didn't want to die with him."

Darren's hand came over hers, and he gave her fingers a gentle squeeze, with the corners of his mouth lifting into an understanding smile. Ellie missed the warmth of his hand when he took it away to change gear, then gripped the wheel again, the cigarette burning away between his fingers.

"I've been lookin' over my shoulder since I picked you up earlier. I dunno how bad he hit his head, the fuckin' maggot," Darren said. "What made you take the gun?"

It was in my hand. I raised it to his head, and I tried to kill him. "I knew he would use it if I left it." She shifted her position in her seat, averting her eyes. "There was only one gun that I could see in the cab. I had to take it."

"Did you train it on him?"

Ellie's hand flew up to her face, her mouth dropping open. She turned to him. "*No.*"

"No?" Darren's eyes narrowed. "You sure?"

He checked the rearview mirror, and then edged the car towards the right-hand fork in the road, the wheels struggling to grip, but he coaxed them with a little power, and the car made a reluctant turn onto the Buckfastleigh road, leaving behind the moorland lane that branched off above them to the left.

Ellie lowered her head, chewing her nails, with her eyes turned away. She felt her breathing quicken as she closed her eyes, picturing the gun in her hand, with Braddon's blood-splashed temple within her sights. Her head lolled as she replayed the scene, each time with her finger poised, her aim perfect, and her finger paralysed.

"Did you point it at him, Ellie?" Darren said.

Her eyes opened as she raised her head, with her mouth downturned, and she swallowed. "Yes, but I couldn't do it. No matter how sadistic he is, I couldn't fire it."

Darren fidgeted. "You had your finger on the trigger?"

"I couldn't pull it. My finger just wouldn't."

Darren took a drag on the cigarette, but it had expired, and he crushed it against the dashboard. He sized her up, and threw the cigarette butt out of the window.

"Could you live with it if you had?"

"I don't know. I came that close, Darren. That close."

"Yeah, I reckoned you had."

Ellie felt her tears build, with the tightness in her throat that hurt when she swallowed. She saw his grim expression through her blurry vision, and she blinked hard, wiping her eyes, gulping down the hard lump in her throat.

"My bro killed a burglar," Darren said, "back in Perth, years ago. The guilt was instant, and he tried to revive him. The bloke was unarmed. It was a bad time for the family, I reckon. We drifted. I came to Britain with an ancestry visa, then kept out of trouble." His mouth hardened into a line. "It worked . . . for a while."

Ellie studied him, with her head against the headrest, as he reduced the wipers to a steady swipe, and then turned down the heater.

"Did you tell Charlotte this when you dated her?" she said.

"Nah." He closed his window and shrugged. "No point. She just wanted a baby. Said she was on the pill, but she lied."

Ellie nodded. "She did the same to another guy, two years ago. She says she doesn't need a man."

"She made that clear."

The road twisted downwards, snow turning to sleet as the car plowed on, the slush spraying up beneath the chassis. He steered right across the road, avoiding a fallen branch, whose sharp twigs scratched the body of the car, with a teeth-grinding squeak, as it scraped passed, Ellie squirming, clamping her teeth together, while the sound shivered right through her.

She jolted as Braddon's face loomed in front of her, taking her breath, until she shut down the image in her mind, and breathed out, with her hands gripping the edge of her seat. She relaxed her grip, and her shoulders sagged.

"Why does Braddon want to hurt me so much?" she whispered. "What did I do?"

Darren glanced over, with his brow creased, and his mouth screwed up. "What?"

"Braddon said I was asking for it. Said that I deserve everything that happens to me. He said it's because of my tight jeans."

"Bollocks. You could have been wearin' anythin', and he'd still come after you. He's a fuckin' deviant, thinks he owns women's bodies. He doesn't think 'no' applies to him."

Ellie looked down, tracing a bruise on the back of her hand with the tip of her finger. "He drugged me, and I couldn't fight him off. Maybe I could have been stronger."

"You need to talk to someone, beaut. You have to get this guilt thing out of your head. None of this is your fault."

Ellie swallowed, turning to see him. "I don't want to talk to anyone."

Darren rubbed his forehead, and he gave a long sigh. "Seriously Ellie, talk to someone, read stuff on the internet, just don't be his victim for the rest of your life." He shook his head. "You had no choice in what he did to you, but you have a choice in how you deal with it."

Ellie watched Darren for a while, studying his profile, the high cheekbones, his strong jaw, his straight nose, and the bruising. She remembered the ardent look in his eye when he made love to her, the strength of his muscles, the wild thrusting inside her, and her deep satisfaction. He didn't seem to notice her watching as he drove, and he didn't hide the look of uneasiness spreading across his face as the town appeared in the murk below them.

"Brett had better be out," he said. "I can't let him see you."

"You let Wade see me."

"Wade isn't Brett."

Ellie stared through the windscreen as huge raindrops smacked against the windscreen in front of her, forming vertical cascades. The wipers scooped them aside, the water merging into a single, rolling wave at the edge of the windscreen, with the shimmering lights of the houses appearing through the glass as the town drew near. *What if Brett's there? What will he do?*

"Is Brett the man who renovated Wade's salon?" she said.

"Yeah, he's doin' up a shit-hole in Buckfastleigh. Makin' it look good, I reckon. There's no alarm fitted," Darren said. "Should be easy."

"You're going to break into a house?" Ellie closed her eyes for a moment, shaking her head, hoping that she'd misunderstood his intention.

His face tightened. "Yeah. What did you think I would do?" he said. "Knock on some bloke's front door, and ask for a room for the night?"

"Oh God, Darren. I can't let you do this." Ellie wrung her hands, "I really can't."

"Yeah, you can. I'll force the window, and give you a leg up."

Ellie cringed, and then shook her head. "No. He may be your friend, but we can't do that to him."

He cursed under his breath, then gave a slight shake of the head. "Look, Ellie, it won't be for long. I'll get the call soon," he said. "If Braddon hadn't shown up at the cottage,"—he shot her sidelong glance—"we'd still be there, rootin' all day and night."

"Rootin'?"

"Shaggin'."

"Oh." Ellie blushed, reddening further as Darren gave her a sudden, wolfish smile.

"I still could, beaut . . . only now it would kill me."

The rain poured as they drove into the town under a darkening sky, the clouds low, and the river high, too high, with sandbags and flood barriers lining the door-ways of dwellings near the river.

Darren scanned the narrow streets before turning into them, with Ellie's head down, and her hands twist-ing in her lap as Darren kerb-crawled, looking for the property, Ellie sneaking a look at him as he leaned towards her and peered through her window. She saw the muscles relax in his face as he drove further along the road, and then pulled up onto the footpath, switching off the engine, with the wipers halting mid-sweep across the windscreen.

He blew out his cheeks, then whistled. "Just made it, fuel's about to run out. Only a couple of miles left in the tank."

Ellie looked up and frowned. "I thought we were parking on the drive."

Darren blinked, his lips parting. "You thought . . ." He shook his head, with a smirk appearing on his lips. "Beaut, I'm breakin' in. Why would I park on the bloody drive?"

Ellie folded her arms, and pursed her mouth, fixing her stare on him. "This is all new to me," she said. "I'm not used to this sort of life, Darren."

"You reckon I am?" He reached for the ignition key, and then froze, staring through the wing mirror, with the colour draining from his face. "*Christ.*"

"What? What is it?" she said.

Ellie turned to look behind, but he gripped her shoulder, and forced her back into her seat, with Ellie wide-eyed as Darren glanced through the rear window, and then swallowed hard.

He returned to the wheel, looking straight ahead, with his face pale, and his body tense as he restarted the engine. Ellie watched his chest rise and fall with each quickened breath, and as he stared into the rear-view mirror, Ellie squeezed his arm.

"Darren, what is it?"

"Braddon."

Oh God, no. No. Ellie clutched at her throat, turning in her seat to look, the heat rushing to her face. "Has he seen us?"

"Oh fuck," he said, "he has now."

CHAPTER ELEVEN

TORRENT

The car screamed in the wrong gear as Darren floored the accelerator, whipping the wheel around, the car lurching off the kerb, banging back down onto the road, as the pickup truck gained fast. Ellie cried out, dazzled by the glare of the headlights through the wing mirror, the cabin floodlit by the sudden flare from the twin spotlights, mounted high on the truck behind. Darren wrenched the gear lever over, the car accelerating, his fingers curled tight around the steering wheel, with his knuckles white, and his eyes wild.

Ellie pressed herself back in her seat, her elbows clamped to her sides, with her fists clenched, and her breath bursting in and out of her. She squeezed her eyes shut tight as the junction hurtled towards her, and she felt the force as Darren braked hard. Ellie's eyes snapped open, and her hands flew up to her mouth when she saw the road closed to the right, the flood barriers barring the way, with nowhere to go but back onto the moors.

"Christ." Darren hit the wheel with the palm of his hand. "We don't have the fuel for this." The car swerved to the left, onto the steep hillside road, as Darren spun the wheel.

Ellie felt a jolt in her stomach, with her throat closing, and her pulse throbbing in her neck. "Don't let him get me. Please don't let him get me." She turned to look behind, but Darren jerked his head.

"Face the front. Don't look at him."

Ellie collapsed into her seat, with her head bowed, and her stomach knotted. The surge flung her backwards as the car soared up the incline, her fists tight in her lap, and her nails drawing blood. Darren braked with his left foot, the hill levelling out, and the car drifting, swaying, with Darren steering, hand over hand, through the sharp bends, the gear changes rapid, acceleration harsh, and his breathing fast. The small car struggled to respond, and the aching pit in Ellie's stomach grew as the truck closed in.

Darren tensed. "Shit, he's gonna ram us."

Ellie braced, with her neck and jaw tight, and the pressure of the headrest hard against the back of her head. The reflected headlight grew in the mirror beside her as the truck advanced, her heart jumping in her chest, and her pulse rapid. The truck collided with the rear of the car, a violent, jarring crash that jolted her forward, the car skidding, Ellie clutching Darren's arm as her choking cry broke free from her throat.

"Darren—"

"Let go. It's OK."

Darren rammed the lever into second, and the car screamed up the hill, skidding sideways into the curves, accelerating straight out of the bends, Darren whipping through the gears, with his eyes focused, and his teeth clenched.

The truck raced up through the mirror, and Ellie jerked upright. "Darren, he's coming again—"

"Shit."

The car swerved as Darren snatched the wheel hard to the right, the truck clipping the rear bumper, pitching the car, the tyres squealing on the rain-soaked road as Ellie's body lurched, her heart drumming against her ribs. The truck's reflection disappeared from her wing mirror as Darren fought for control, and as Ellie turned in her seat, looking back, the truck swerved towards the driver's side, then accelerated, scraping alongside, drawing level.

Darren snapped his head around. "Jesus *Christ*."

He yanked Ellie's head down as Braddon fired the gun into the car, Ellie screaming as Darren's window shattered, showering his legs with glass, with the rain pouring in, and the bullet lodging in the door beside her. She cowered, with her trembling hands pressed against the side of her head, Ellie deafened by her screams.

Darren made an extreme hard turn on the steering wheel, forcing the car down a tiny cart track. The car shuddered through the water-filled wheel ruts, with the chassis scraping along the grassy ridge between them, the rough walls closing in on either side, and the sound of the engine echoing back from the stonework.

The growl of the truck died away, the cabin of the car dimmed, and Ellie looked back through the misted rear window, her chin quivering, the truck backing out of the narrow track behind them, turning, racing onwards along the hill road, disappearing behind the high bank of trees above them.

"Where is he?" Darren whipped his head around, searching the mirrors, ducking his head to see the top of the bank. "Where did he go?"

"I don't know. He backed off. The track's too narrow." Ellie hung on as the car pitched and rocked over the rough ground. "He carried on."

Darren pointed to the hill. "Up there?" he said. "Is that where he went?"

Ellie nodded. "He was driving fast."

"Shit, he'll try to cut us off."

Darren gasped as he glanced down, slowing the car, steering one-handed, with his other hand on his thigh, and a dazed look in his eyes. Ellie caught her breath as the blood seeped through the leg of his jeans and she unclipped her seatbelt, reaching out to him, the fear spearing her gut as he glanced over with pain in his eyes.

"Are you Ok?" she said. "Let me look."

"Beaut, sit back. I need to turn the car."

"Darren, you're bleeding. You need to stop."

Ellie snatched a cloth from the glove box, wrapping it around her hand, scooping up the slivers of glass from his jeans, while holding onto the dashboard as the car bumped over the ruts.

Darren struggled to drive, with the blood welling up through a small tear in his jeans, and then leaking onto his fingers. "Jeeze. I need to get this glass out."

He leaned forward, squinting through the rain, edging the car through a narrow gateway, and onto a gravel patch hidden by the close-growing trees, the car skidding as he dragged on the handbrake. The engine cut out as the rain spattered onto him through the smashed window, with dark splashes appearing on his blue jeans. He tipped his head back, panting, his eyes dull with pain.

Ellie took his hand from his thigh, flinching at the sight of the small shard of glass embedded in his flesh, and she gulped. "Do you want me to pull it out?"

"No." He grasped her hand to stop her. "I'll do it."

Ellie's toes curled inside her boots as Darren held open the tear in his jeans, taking the glass between his thumb and fingers, and then drawing a long breath before easing out the shard, bit by bit, his lip curled, with blood oozing out of the cut. He threw the shard into the foot well, and slapped his hand over the wound, holding out his other hand for the cloth.

Ellie shook her head. "It's full of glass. Sorry, I didn't think."

"Bloody hell."

Darren's shoulders sagged, and his eyes closed for a moment before he gave a small shake of the head, and then tugged the gun from the door pocket, unwrapped the oil-streaked rag from around it, and then folded the rag into a pad.

Ellie gasped, reaching for the rag. "You can't use that. It's filthy."

Darren fended her off and held the rag against his thigh. "Beaut, don't fuss."

He replaced the gun, and drew out his phone, slipping it into his back pocket. He pressed down on the rag, his expression grim as he wiped his bloodied hand on his sweater.

Ellie glanced passed him at the rain splashing over the windowsill into the car, feeling the spray on her forearm, and the tight knot in her throat.

"What's going to happen to us if Braddon's waiting at the end of the track?" She turned her gaze on him as she heard him draw breath. "This little car won't take much more, Darren."

"I know how it bloody feels."

He reached forward, turning the ignition key. The engine fired, then spluttered, before cutting out, with a strong smell of fuel entering the cabin through the vents. He tried the key again, pumping the accelerator, but the engine failed to start.

He slumped over the wheel with a groan, resting his forehead on his hands. "Jesus."

Ellie clutched at her throat, holding her breath as he turned the key, over and over, until the hum of the heater dropped in tone, and the headlights dimmed, as the car battery lost power. Darren sat back with a long, deep sigh, then flicked the key. The wipers worked once, with the gravelled clearing appearing through the windscreen, and then the scene vanished as the rain poured, and the windows misted over.

Ellie choked back a sob, with her stomach churning, and a heavy feeling in her chest. She felt Darren's cold hand close over hers, and as she met his eyes, he stroked her cheek, and gave her a weak smile.

"End of the line, darlin'. Time to go." He leaned over and opened the door. "Wait for me."

Darren limped through the rain, holding the rag against his thigh, with the gun hanging from his other hand. Ellie sat still, watching him with an ache beneath her breastbone as he stumbled. He motioned to her, and she joined him, the rain pelting her face, drenching her jeans as she screwed up her eyes against the rain, and nodded towards the gun.

"Would you use it if you had to?" she said.

"Can't." He limped passed her, heading for the rear of the car. "It's not loaded."

"What?" Ellie's gaze followed him.

"No bullets." Darren lifted the lid of the boot and peered inside. "You wouldn't have shot him if you'd pulled the trigger."

Ellie stared. "How long have you known that?"

"Since you gave it to me." He looked over at her, and then shrugged. "You saw me check it. I reckon Braddon wasn't takin' any chances." He rummaged in the boot, and pulled out a length of cable. "Come here."

Ellie's heart thumped in her chest as she eyed him, with the boot open, and the gun perched on the edge of it, the cable flexing within his hands as Darren stared her down. His brow creased as he glanced at the cable, and then at the boot before he looked back at her, with his mouth downturned, and his arms by his side.

"For Christ's sake, Ellie."

"I thought—"

"I'm tyin' it around my bloody leg. What the hell did you think I was doin'?"

Ellie breathed out and splashed through the rain towards him, with her ears reddening, and her head down. She crouched in front of him, averting her gaze, holding the rag tight against his thigh as he wound the cable around it and anchored the makeshift pad in place. Before he straightened up, he put his mouth to her ear, his face stern.

"I didn't shag you for the hell of it. I've got a bloody soft spot for you, and I'm not gonna tie you up and force you into the friggin' boot." He pulled her up, picked up the gun, and slammed the boot shut. "Come on."

He led her at an alarming pace along the muddy path, between the trees, as rainwater flowed down the natural gullies at the edge of the incline, Ellie sweeping her wet hair off her face as the droplets ran down her cheeks. The pain gnawed deep inside her ankle as she tried to keep up with him.

"Please slow down," she said. "I can't keep up."

He glanced back, his eyes full of pain, and his breathing as harsh as her own. "You can, darl'. Keep with me."

"But I'm hurting."

"I know, beaut. It won't be for long."

"Promise?"

Her knees jolted with every step as he rushed her onwards, Darren's hand against his ribs, his limp pronounced as he forced his way through the nettles growing over the path, the stingers springing back against Ellie's thighs as she passed through, her sharp gasps inaudible over the rain.

"I can hear the river. It's not far," Darren said without turning. "The path runs alongside, and it's our only way back into town. He can't follow us in the pickup."

Ellie heard the roar of the river, and she slackened her pace, panting, with her hand to her chest as he strode onwards. "But that hill road," she said, "leads up through these woods. I can see the whole track that we drove along from up here." She raised her voice as the distance increased between them. "He'll know that we've stopped, and he could be anywhere, waiting for us . . . and he could have laid traps."

She saw his shoulders tense from behind, with a falter in his step, and then he slowed down, reaching for her hand as she caught up with him, and he tugged her onwards. He took the right-hand fork in the path, heading deeper into the woods, the ancient oak trees gnarled, with trunks coated in lichen, and moss cloaking their protruding roots.

The path narrowed into a tiny rabbit track, weaving between the oaks, and as Ellie stepped over the mass of tangled roots, she struck her head against a low-slung branch above her, stumbling into him, yelling out. She clutched him, Darren wavering, holding her steady as Ellie held her head, with her teeth clenched.

"Why didn't you duck?" He stroked her tousled hair. "I thought you'd seen it."

"I was looking down. I thought there may be traps." The shock and pain subsided as he placed a protective arm around her shoulders. "I . . . I was frightened of stepping on one . . ."

"Oh mate." He wrapped his strong arms around her, holding her tight, his chest against hers, and the rough bristles on his chin against her temple. "There are no traps, darl'."

Ellie gazed up into his eyes as he studied her face, then he dipped his head, dropping a kiss on her flushed lips.

Ellie jumped as Darren's phone rang and then it cut off, Darren snatching it from his back pocket, with his arm around her. He studied the screen, swiping over the crack in the glass, Ellie trying to see, but he held the phone at an angle, and Ellie's chin trembled.

"Why won't you let me look?" she said.

"There's nothin' to see, beaut. It's just a missed call."

His eyes narrowed as a message betrayed its arrival with a bleep, and Ellie pulled his arm down to see the screen, with her hand fastening around his wrist. The message opened with a single swipe of his finger across the rain-spattered screen, and he jerked his arm free from Ellie's grasp, throwing her a pained look before reading the message himself. She watched him read it through once more before he turned the phone off, lowering his hand, with his eyes closed. He swallowed, pushing the phone into his back pocket, and then looked down at her, his voice soft.

"Ransom's paid, beaut."

Ellie reeled. Her eyes closed, and her body wavered. She wanted to feel relief, to feel free, but as she opened her eyes, and stared up at him, she didn't feel anything, just a hard lump lodged in her throat and a tight grip across her chest.

"I'm . . . I'm free to go?" she said.

"Yeah . . . I reckon."

Ellie's heart lurched, a chill shuddering through her bones, and she clutched his arm. "Darren, don't leave me on my own in here. Please don't just abandon me."

"Don't fret, beaut. I'll get you home—"

"Oh my God." Ellie jerked, with her hands racing to her mouth, and her eyes wide. "Braddon knows where I live. He'll find me. You said that the ransom won't stop him—"

"Oh, Jesus." Darren scraped his fingers through his hair, with a dazed look in his eyes. "I didn't think of that."

"He knows where you live too. He tracked you," she said. "What are we going to do?"

"Trust me, beaut. I'll think of somethin'."

He took her hand, leading her onwards through the twisted oaks, the rumble of distant thunder drowning out the roar of the rushing water as they neared the river. The track broadened and swung away to the left, but he led her to the edge of the wood, and pulled her forwards, over the grass, with the mud squelching underfoot.

The river of whitewater swirled below them, roaring downstream, the spray forming a mist that hung in the air, with the surrounding hillside grey and foreboding. A curtain of rain fell across the valley floor, and the sudden flash of lightening blinded her, the thunder clap echoing around the hills, vibrating in her chest, and she tightened her grip on his hand, his fingers curling tight around hers.

Darren pulled her back from the edge, pointing to the swollen river. "If we can get down there, we can get away."

"Darren, the riverside path has gone. It's submerged." Ellie drew closer to him. "And if we could find a way through," she said, "how do we get down to the river?"

Darren faltered, biting the inside of his cheek as he looked up and downstream. "Dunno. It's a thirty-foot drop, I reckon. It's not so bad over there." He nodded towards the right. "We'll climb down and see how we go." He let go of her hand, and Ellie tugged his arm.

"But it's so steep. We should try the left. There are rocks jutting out to hold onto, look." She pointed, then lowered her hand, frowning.

Mud and water trickled over the protruding rocks just below the top of the bank, and as she peered over the edge in front of her, another rivulet of muck and water forced its way through, bigger, and faster. More earth broke away, further down, rocks loosening, rolling, and Ellie backed into him, clutching his arm with her trembling hand, holding her breath.

"Christ," Darren yelled. "The bank's givin' way."

There came a resounding crack from behind, and as Ellie looked back in horror, the earth bulged beneath her feet, with an eerie sucking sound of oozing, moving mud. With a brutal jolt, the ground broke away as the bank tore itself apart behind them, plunging them into the raging torrent below.

The force dragged her under, her rigid body racing down into a pit of darkness, her lungs choking, emptying, with a mass of bubbles escaping her mouth, her ears filling with water, the sounds muffled, time slowing as the weight of her jacket pulled her down.

His hand clamped around her throat, dragging her upwards, her head piercing the surface, with the rain on her face, and a roar in her ears, her lungs gasping for air. She went under again, sounds muted, and then he hauled her up, Ellie floundering, her lungs burning, with the sound of the crashing river loud in her ears, the thunder rolling, and rain spattering onto her face.

Darren clung onto a protruding branch hanging low in the water, with his hand around her throat, keeping her head above the surface. His lips moved, and she heard his shout over the noise of the thundering river, surging over the rocks around them.

"I couldn't hold you . . . I've got you now."

The weight of the rushing water pulled her feet from under her, but Darren hooked his arm around her, gripping the branch above him with his bloodied arm, his sweater torn from shoulder to wrist, and his taut muscles rippling with the strain as he pulled himself along the branch.

Ellie felt her body cramping, the ice-cold water chilling her veins, Darren gasping, his teeth clenched as he dragged himself up, hauling her with him, out of the swirling mass, and onto higher ground, sheltered by the trees growing close to the edge.

Ellie fell against him, her chest pitching and falling as she gulped the air, her shaking limbs weak and chilled, with the water seeping from her clothes onto the ground beneath her. She felt his hand slip beneath her chin as he lifted her head, and she glimpsed his dishevelled figure through her watery eyes, with an ache in her throat as she saw his vacant expression, the gash to his forearm, and the blood on his jeans.

He felt her pulse, Ellie's sobs escaping from her throat as she gasped for breath. He held her against him until she calmed, Ellie soothed by the warmth of his body. He nodded towards the broken branches and debris, sweeping under the stone bridge downstream.

"That could have been us." His voice cracked. "I didn't think I could hold you."

Ellie tipped her head on one side, eyeing him as he glanced down at her with his sorrowful eyes, the rain rinsing the mud from his hair, diluting the blood that trickled down his forearm. She touched his bruised cheek as he shivered.

He held her close, with her face against the soft skin of his neck, his pulse beating against her cheek. Ellie put her hand on his chest, her eyes opening wide as she felt the flutter beneath her palm as he breathed. She pushed herself up, then wiped the blood from his cheek with her sleeve, Darren's breathing laboured.

"You're hurt," Ellie said. "You can't hide it from me."

"Don't worry about me, Ellie . . . I'll be OK."

Ellie wrapped her arms around him, holding him close, stroking his back as he lowered his head, his hands around her waist, and his cheek against hers. Ellie closed her eyes, listening to his rasping breaths, feeling his pain.

She felt him lurch, his body tensing, and as Ellie turned, she zeroed in on the figure appearing out of the mist in the middle distance, with a gun in his hand, and a rifle slung across his back. The tendons tightened in Ellie's neck, her mouth open, crying out, with her heart lurching.

Darren yelled out, dragging Ellie to her feet as Jon Braddon raised the handgun, with both of his hands to the trigger. The gun wavered. The sharp crack echoed around the hillside as blood spattered across Darren's neck and jawbone, the bullet embedding itself within his shoulder. Darren howled, staggering backwards into the river, dragging Ellie with him as she clung to him, screaming.

Pains radiated through Ellie's chest, with ice-cold water surging over her head as she grappled for his wrist, her fingers digging into his flesh, her arm pulling tight as she held onto him, gripping the overhanging branch with her free hand, jerking her head up, Darren struggling to keep his above water.

Ellie choked back her sobs as she struggled to hold him, the force of the current twisting him from her grasp, his fingers slipping from her wrist. She clutched at him as he let go, her screams echoing as Darren was swept away by the river that raged around him like a demon on its way to the sea.

CHAPTER TWELVE

BAIT

Ellie clung to the branch, her sobs bursting from her chest, with a hollow void spreading through her gut, her stomach caving in, and her heart crumbling. She turned her eyes to Braddon, coming closer, the gun in his hand, with a jagged hunter's knife, dangling from his utility belt, bouncing against his leg with each slow step towards her.

Ellie clutched at her chest, pains shooting with each shallow gasp, and heat mounting between her legs as her urine dribbled down the inside of her jeans, her calves cramping as the icy river tugged and pulled.

Her grip tightened around the branch as she heaved herself onto the bank, with her legs dangling in the water, Ellie slipping, clawing at the grass, dragging herself out of the river.

Braddon was closer now, with his solid frame widening as he pulled back his shoulders, his chest thrust out, with his lips flattened, and his eyes hard. His hand slid down to the knife, unhooking it from its carabiner, his broken fingers, awkward, curling around the handle. His other arm crossed his body as he slipped the handgun into his belt.

Oh God, no. Ellie's shoulders curved inwards, with tiny whimpers emitting from her closed throat. *Darren, why did you leave me? I need you. Darren, I really need you.* Her eyes filled with tears, with a weight pressing down on her ribcage. Her hand brushed the pocket of her jacket, feeling Darren's watch stowed inside, and her face crumpled, with tears trickling over the edge of her lower eyelids.

Braddon bore down on her, Ellie scrambling to her feet, her knees buckling, with the wet jacket sagging, weighing her down as she fled, weaving through the trees, following the river downstream, with her jaw slack, and her hands curled into fists.

He crashed through the undergrowth behind her, his military boots thudding the sodden earth, with Ellie's lungs bursting. She looked back, Braddon's bloodied nostrils streaming, his eyes evil, with saliva on his lips, and his teeth bared. He grabbed at her hair, Ellie squealing, snatching her head forward, with her chest heaving, and her gaze jerking from scene to scene as her legs shook beneath her.

She forced her way through the vegetation, running blind, gaining distance as his breathing rasped, Braddon snorting and spitting, slowing down behind her.

Fallen branches barred her way, with the trees closing in, and the muddy tracks indistinct beneath a carpet of dead leaves. She tripped and fell, rolling downward into a pit of brambles, Ellie lying prostrate, with her foot caught in a snaking vine, and her body stung all over by the nettles.

Something shifted in the undergrowth above her and Ellie scrambled to her feet, snatching a long, jagged stick from the ground, her mouth open, with a whimper dying in her throat as Braddon stood over her, on the edge of the bank, staring down at her with the gun trained between her eyes.

"Try to run now, you fucking bitch."

"You killed Darren, you bastard," Ellie yelled. "He was your first human kill, wasn't he? Did it give you a thrill, like you thought it would?" Ellie flinched as he narrowed his eyes, the gun wavering. "Kill me, Jon. Pull the trigger."

Braddon flicked the catch and lowered the gun, a smirk appearing on his cruel lips as he pushed the gun into his belt, and drew out the knife. He dropped down to her with a thud, and seized her shoulder, twisting her around, thrusting his arm around her neck, with the knife against her throat.

"You'll die on my terms, Ell," he whispered. "Like that bastard face down in the river."

Braddon licked her ear, pushing his hot, wet tongue deep inside, Ellie squirming, pulling at his arm as the knife pushed against her skin. His hand slid between her legs, and as he groped her, Ellie fought the tears.

The stick chafed against the palm of her hand as she tightened her fist, with the sharp jagged end of the stick pointing upwards. Ellie twisted her arm, turning the stick, holding her breath, with her eyes screwed tight as Braddon forced his hand into her jeans, his breath nauseating as he breathed against her cheek. Ellie jerked, gritting her teeth, as he jabbed his fingers inside her.

She gripped the stick like a dagger, thrusting it into his face. The sharp point speared his eye, digging into the black iris, and gouging a trench through the white, the stick breaking off in Ellie's hand. The blood and clear, gel-like goo spattered over his cheek, Ellie's stomach turning over. Braddon screamed, and fell against the bank, cowering as he clutched at the stick lodged in his eye.

Ellie launched herself from his hold, and scrambled up the bank, gasping for air. She looked back as she reached the top, gagging as he plucked the twig from his eye, Braddon howling, clear goo hanging in threads from the end of the stick, mixing with blood. Braddon crouched, his hands curled into claws, and his lips snarling, with his face and neck blood red, and the vein throbbing at his temple. His body tensed, on the verge of springing, and Ellie's heart jolted. *Oh Christ, run.*

Braddon scrambled up the incline, Ellie fleeing, wild, erratic, her muscles rigid, Ellie running for her life. Nettles hanging from branches above snatched at her hair, scraping her face, Ellie sobbing, ripping her hair free of the cruel barbs, strands of her hair breaking at the roots as the sound of Braddon's coarse breathing neared.

Ellie screamed, lurching away from a rusting animal trap lying in wait, inches from her toes, with its jaws open, half-buried in the leaves. Ellie staggered, tripping, falling onto her knees, stones digging into her shins as her legs missed the trap by a mere inch or two.

She struggled to her feet, reeling as the trap snapped shut around Braddon's lower leg as he lunged for her, the teeth ripping open his skin through his trousers, his bones fracturing, the blood spurting, soaking his boot. He crashed to the ground, crying out, gagging and writhing, his face twisted, with the hunter's knife wedged in his arm, the rifle sliding to the ground.

He gasped, reaching out to her. "Ell, help me."

Ellie shuddered as fluid dribbled onto his cheek from his lacerated eye, the bones in his leg cracking, and splintering as he edged himself towards her, his face twisting as he squirmed, clutching at his trapped limb with his broken hand, his jaw clenching.

"Ell, I need help. Give me your hand."

Ellie's heart lurched, and her stomach knotted, her hands clutching her throat. *Oh shit. Oh shit.* She stepped forward, and then backed off, with her mind split in two.

"Help me, you little fucker," he yelled.

Ellie backed right off, and Braddon snatched the handgun from beneath him, the barrel wavering as he pointed it at her. He fired the gun, the mud and grass spattering over her boots as the bullet hit the ground in front of her toes, Ellie squealing. Braddon yanked at the trap, Ellie's eyes widening as the trap moved, working loose from its anchor, his lips snarling.

Ellie lunged forward, seizing the rifle from the ground, turning it in her hands, heavy, awkward, its butt facing downward as she raised the gun above her head. She smashed the butt across the bridge of his nose, bone and gristle collapsing, Braddon slumping sideways, gurgling, with blood running over his lips, and across his face, Ellie gasping. The gun in his hand lifted, Braddon training it on her chest, releasing the catch, the trigger squeezing beneath his fingers.

Ellie raised the rifle again, her hands clammy, the rifle slipping from her grip as she ploughed the butt into the side of his head, the corner driving into his temple, his body lurching. He lay, twitching, the handgun falling, Ellie's eyes bulging.

She staggered back, whimpering, gasping, pains squeezing her chest as Braddon lay broken, and bleeding. His breathing slowed, and Ellie vomited as the life drained from him, Braddon still, staring out through eyes as soulless as when he was alive. Ellie ripped up a handful of grass and threw it on the ground beside his broken face, but no breath stirred it until the wind caught it, and blew it across his body, the blades sticking to his blood.

Ellie stood still, her eyes wet, and her face hot, sweating. She wanted to feel relief, to feel justice for Darren, and for the girls in the videos, but pain instead came in place of these things, and she glanced at her bloodstained jacket, and then looked down at the bloodied rifle in her hands. Ellie staggered. *Oh, God.*

The river roared in the distance, and Ellie took to her heels, running, and slipping, her legs floundering in the undergrowth as she pulled Darren's watch from her jacket, then crammed it into the pocket of her jeans.

She wedged the rifle under her arm, and dragged down the zip of her jacket, tugging as the teeth jammed. She yanked hard, breaking the zip, and peeled off the jacket, folding it around the rifle, with her heart thudding, and her hands shaking. She approached the river, her gaze darting upstream, and then down, Ellie stumbling over logs and debris that lined the edge of the swollen river, with the cold wind finding its way beneath her sweater.

She didn't dare look for Darren's body. Ellie pictured him, floating, face down, his face blue-grey, and his eyes swollen, blind eyes staring down into the depths of the river, like the body she'd seen last year, pulled from the sea by the surfers she'd flirted with moments earlier. His body bloated, with blood that once surged through his veins, now still, with a blue tinge to his tanned skin. She choked back her tears and pushed the image away.

She heaved the gun and the jacket into the fast-flowing water, and as they clattered over the rocks, Ellie backed away, standing in the shadows of the trees. She wiped the sweat from her face as she waited for the jacket to bob up again, but it stayed beneath the surface, and a single sob fled from her.

Her hands were bloody, and she darted forward, kneeling, leaning over, rinsing her hands in the rushing water, splashing her face, and wiping the blood from the ends of her hair. Ellie scrambled to her feet and turned away, shivering, with her hand in her pocket, clutching Darren's watch.

She froze, hearing the growl of a vehicle heading uphill, the sound changing as Ellie watched the rescue truck driving at speed across the stone bridge, further downstream. Ellie traced its imagined route with her eyes until it reappeared between low stone walls, Ellie hurrying forwards, heading for the road. *They'll stop to help me. They'll have to. I'll say I fell into the river. It's not a lie.*

She clambered over the fallen trees, brought down by the torrent, her hands scratched and bleeding, her injured ankle throbbing as her pains returned, and her body shuddering as the biting wind tore through her.

The rescue truck came into view as it headed for the hairpin bend, Ellie scrambling over the wall, running out, waving. The truck took the bend wide, and as it veered around the corner, on the wrong side of the road, Ellie froze.

The truck ploughed into her leg, her bones cracking, and deforming, with her screams drowning out the screech of tyres as she hit the ground. The hot rod of pain burned from her toes up to her scalp, as she lay like a ragdoll on the asphalt, with her leg twisted out of shape beneath her. The cold, dark state of unconsciousness crept into her vision and blacked out her mind.

CHAPTER THIRTEEN

SILHOUETTE

The coffee shop buzzed with university students and retired ladies, all vying for a plump sofa or the few cosy window seats overlooking the picturesque river, and the church on the opposite bank. A chaotic surge of people pushed their way in through the doorway, a hurried crowd from the office across the road.

Ellie didn't look up, perched in the middle of her favourite window seat, on a plump fitted cushion, with her leg outstretched, encased in a heavy plaster cast, resting on the chair nearest to her. The crutches leaned against the wall beside her, with her winter coat folded into a neat bundle on the other chair.

She eased the hem of her tight woollen skirt down her thighs a little as the draught blew in through the door, and she hitched up her long woollen sock, covering her knee, just above her knee-length boot. She wriggled her bare toes of her other foot for warmth as she couldn't reach them.

She didn't want company, preferring to be alone with her smartphone, browsing a million and one websites for flights and university courses, anything that would take her out of the country she loved, to a place where she could move on.

She glanced at her empty coffee cup on the table, and as she caught the eye of the barista, Ellie nodded, and he came over with a fresh latte, smiling and eyeing her up. Ellie forced a smile and passed him her credit card along with her loyalty card. He lingered a little when he returned to her table, but Ellie took her cards and gave her thanks without looking at him, her shoulders sagging and her head shaking as he walked away.

She took a sip of coffee, wrinkled her nose, and then heaped a spoonful of sugar into the cup, stirring, staring into the swirling milk, swirling like whitewater in the river. She shivered and dropped the spoon onto the table with a clatter, glancing at her phone.

A shadow fell across the screen. That new barista was becoming a pest. *Will he ever leave me alone?* She shifted the phone but the shadow persisted, following, and as Ellie switched off the screen and gave a deep sigh, she caught sight of the silver biker buckle on the belt of his jeans. The table jerked, her latte spilling, as she looked up into Darren's eyes.

"Oh my God." She clutched at the table, her breath stalling and her jaw dropping.

"How ya goin', beaut?" Darren gave her a steady smile and placed his take-out cup on the table, reaching for the paper napkins. He mopped the spillage, one handed, with his other arm in a sling, and the sleeve of his leather jacket tucked in at the shoulder.

Ellie couldn't take her eyes off him as her thoughts chased one another in circles, with her face burning and she gripped his arm. "Oh God, Darren. I thought . . ."

Darren dropped the sopping napkins onto the floor, kicking them under the window seat, and he shook his head. "Nah, beaut. I got out further downstream. A bunch of hikers pulled me out."

Ellie's eyes widened. "But you could have drowned. You let go of my hand."

He lowered his voice and leaned in. "Had to, beaut. You were a sittin' duck, and you would have been killed. He was comin' for you."

Ellie swallowed and nodded, her eyes downcast. "I ran, but he caught me, and he would have shot me. I had to stop him," she whispered.

"Yeah, I know." He cleared his throat. "Mind if I sit down?"

Ellie looked up and nodded, turning towards him as he slung her coat onto the floor and pulled up the chair, his knee touching her thigh, and his hand on her plaster cast.

"They found him a few days ago," he said, "when I was lyin' in Derriford Hospital waitin' to be discharged. I saw it on the news. Didn't say who he was, but I reckon I know what happened . . ." He patted her plaster cast. "What's goin' on with this then?"

She touched his hand, the heat rising through her body until it burned her cheeks. "I was run over by a rescue truck. I was panicking. I'd done something so bad that I just couldn't think straight."

He leaned forward and whispered in her ear. "No one would blame you for what you did, beaut. I don't." He kissed her cheek and leaned back, reaching for her latte, pushing it towards her.

Ellie pushed the cup away, a squeezing sensation within her throat as she took his hand in hers, the cuts to his knuckles healing, with his hand warm against her palm. "I didn't think I'd see you again. I kept thinking of you, face down . . ." She shivered. "What happened to you?"

"It was touch and go. People surface three times before they stay under, and I was on my third go when the hikers found me," he said. "I heaved my guts up. God knows what was in the water. I blacked out a few times after that. I know that I was stretchered off the hill, and then I remember fightin' off an oxygen mask." He rolled his eyes. "I was a bad patient, I reckon." He looked at her with those captivating eyes. "I remember tellin' a medic that you were in the river, and he phoned through to someone," he said. "They said I'd got him around the throat, yellin' in his face, but I don't remember. I reckon I blacked out again, 'cos the next thing, I was in a hospital with medics askin' me my name. I'd lost gallons of blood you know."

Ellie's mouth dropped open. "You told them about me, and they sent a truck for me?" she whispered. "I was run over by my own rescue team?"

"Oh beaut, you're an unlucky bugger." He gave her a rueful smile.

Ellie touched the sling around his arm. "Did they get the bullet out of your shoulder?"

"Yeah, after diggin' around a bit. It's lyin' in a dish somewhere, probably with forensics proddin' at it."

Ellie stiffened. "If they link it to his gun, they'll think that you killed—"

"Yeah. I thought that too . . ." He cleared his throat. "That's why I'm here. I've come to say 'bye. I fly home to Australia tomorrow. I'm gettin' out of here."

Ellie's heart bumped hard, her throat closing, and as she gazed into his eyes, he took her hand in his again and looked down at her fingers. Ellie swallowed.

"Do you think they'll arrest you, for what I did?" she said.

"Dunno. Truth is that I daren't stay in Britain. Lloyd's a dangerous bloke, and I know too much. So do you. I can disappear in Oz, though that's harder than it used to be, I reckon."

"What will you do out there?"

"Dunno, I'll think of somethin'." He shrugged and then winced, raising his hand to his shoulder. "Shit."

"Doug's treated me to a brand new car and an apartment overlooking the river." She pointed to the beautiful building across the water, but Darren kept his eyes on her. "He's even paid for a hypnotherapist to help me," she said.

Darren raised an eyebrow. "Paid you to keep quiet?"

"Yes, but I'm suffering with nightmares and flashbacks. The guilt's really bad some days, and I know what you said about that, but sometimes I just can't shake it off."

"Flashbacks? I had some in hospital. Thought I was goin' crazy."

"I was taken to the hospital in Exeter. I stayed overnight." She placed her hand on his leg, his muscle hard beneath her palm, and Darren's eyes lit up. "I'm sorry about your watch," she said.

"My watch?" he said.

"It was in my pocket when the truck hit me. I landed on the watch and broke it."

"No worries." He shook his head. "I've given up divin', not too keen on water right now."

"I've given up my journalism course. I didn't think it would be the best job to have, considering Lloyd's profession."

"Yeah, nah. He'd hound you. He won't pay me Braddon's share. I got F–all." The milkshake machine behind him clattered, crushing ice, and he frowned, leaning towards her, raising his voice. "What will you do now?"

Ellie waited until the noise died down, and the customers' voices returned to their normal pitch before she shrugged a little. "I'm taking a year off, but, after what's happened to me, I'm thinking of training as a psychologist, to help other people."

"You've already helped his future victims, beaut. There's one less bastard to harm girls. You'll make it, 'cos you're a fighter. I knew that from the second you kicked that maggot in the bollocks, at the start of all this shit."

Ellie smiled and touched his tidy hair. "You look a lot different since the last time I saw you."

Darren moved his hand to the thigh of her uninjured leg, with his fingertips hidden beneath the hem of her short skirt. "I've had a shower if that's what you mean." He gave her an easy grin and took a quick look over his shoulder before he turned back, with that sudden mischievous glint in his eyes. "Pity that leg of yours is in plaster, and I'm sleepin' on my mate's sofa tonight," he whispered. "I could have taken you back to my place for a soapy root in the shower and then an all-night session, shaggin' in bed, before I fly out in the mornin'."

Ellie gasped, her nipples hardening beneath her clingy top. "Oh, Darren. You really would, wouldn't you?"

"'Course I would." He flicked her hair from out of her eyes. "Beaut, give me your phone number. We'll keep in touch, yeah?"

Ellie scrabbled for her phone as he tugged his own from his pocket, a phone she didn't recognise – a clean smartphone, with a background photo of a Harley Davidson. Ellie unlocked her own phone, the background photo of her cat wearing a party hat appearing, Ellie cringing a little. He took her phone from her, grinning, with his eyebrow raised, and she let him take her number, her new address, and all of her own contact details as she gazed at his short designer stubble, his chiselled jaw, and his soft brown eyes.

He turned his head and caught her watching. "Listen, beaut. Look me up whenever you're in Western Australia."

"How will I find you?"

"You will."

His eyes were intense as he leaned forward, placing his hand to the side of her head. He stroked her cheekbone with his thumb as he watched her, Ellie's body quivering. He gave her a lingering kiss, with his lips soft and his familiar taste on her tongue, and as she breathed in his scent, she knew she would never forget him. He kissed her again and then rose to his feet, touching her cheek.

"I've got to go, darl'. I'll see you sometime." He walked to the door, and then he turned and winked before he walked out, and disappeared into the crowd.

Ellie blinked, with her eyes damp. Moments later, her phone pinged in her trembling hand, and as she looked down, a message appeared on her screen from an unknown number. She swiped it open, her cheeks flushing, her breath catching, and her stomach fluttering as she read the message. *Hi Ellie, I'm here when you need me. Daz*. She breathed in, smiled, and typed her reply.

A NOTE FROM THE AUTHOR

Hi! I'm L.J. Kane. Thanks for reading Captor
Captive. If you've enjoyed the book, please leave a
review on Amazon, and tell your friends!

Coming soon…
Look out for Hunter Hunted
by L.J. Kane,
the Captor Captive sequel due out soon!

I would love to connect with you.
To get the latest info on what I'm up to, follow me on
Twitter: https://twitter.com/L_J_Kane_Author

To follow my blog:
http://ljkaneauthor.wordpress.com/blog

All the best,

L.J. Kane